"They're so beautiful."

Shay gazed at the blossoms that cascaded in white masses against a green backdrop of leaves.

"I'll pick you a bouquet." Eric opened the truck door and stepped to the ground.

"Oh, but they have thorns," she said. "You'll get scratched!"

"Who's afraid of a few thorns!" He was smiling at her. His eyes were such a deep green that they were like dark mirrors reflecting the image of the blackberry blossoms. . . .

Dear Reader,

At Silhouette we publish books with you in mind. We're pleased to announce the creation of Silhouette First Love, a new line of contemporary romances written by the finest young-adult writers as well as outstanding new authors in this field.

Silhouette First Love captures many of the same elements enjoyed by Silhouette Romance readers—love stories, happy endings and the same attention to detail and description. But First Love features young heroines and heroes in contemporary and recognizable situations.

You play an important part in our future plans for First Love. We welcome any suggestions or comments on our books and I invite you to write to us at the address below.

Karen Solem
Editor-in-Chief
Silhouette Books
P.O. Box 769
New York, N.Y. 10019

A SECRET PLACE
Dorothy Francis

First Love from Silhouette

Published by Silhouette Books New York

America's Publisher of Contemporary Romance

Other First Loves by Dorothy Francis

New Boy in Town
Special Girl
Say Please!

SILHOUETTE BOOKS, a Simon & Schuster Division of
GULF & WESTERN CORPORATION
1230 Avenue of the Americas, New York, N.Y. 10020

ISBN: 0-671-53327-4

First Silhouette Books printing September, 1982

10 9 8 7 6 5 4 3 2 1

For Sandy Yeo Smith,
who knows about Tulsa
and Blackberry Winter

1

Shay Stuart smoothed her jeans and cinched her leather belt more tightly around her slim waist before she slipped into her lavender cord jacket.

"Meet you outside, okay?" Mollie McNamara called to her.

"Be right there, Mollie." Shay brushed wispy blond bangs from her eyes in a gesture that had become habit since she had decided to let her bangs grow. Towe Williams liked long hair, and she always tried to please him. It was a miracle that Towe had even given her a second glance, let alone asked her to go steady. If he disliked her bangs, then they had to go.

All around her kids laughed and shouted to one another as they tossed books into lockers, and hallway traffic flowed toward the exit like a suddenly undammed stream. Standing on tiptoe, Shay pulled her math book from the top shelf of her locker and tucked it under her arm. Then she gave her locker door a hurrah-it's-Friday slam and hurried from the chalk-dust-smelling room into the freshness of the early-May afternoon.

"Hey, what took you so long?" Mollie offered Shay a

7

lemon drop, falling in step with her as they crossed the school grounds.

"Towe had to talk to Miss Rice after history class, and I waited for him."

"Beth and Sue have gone on ahead to save us a booth at the D&D."

"Oh."

Shay smiled, hating to break a date with Mollie, who had been her best friend ever since the Stuarts had moved to Tulsa last fall. But Towe came first. Mollie would understand. She and Mollie could go to the Dari-Delite anytime.

Shay liked Mollie, liked to be with her. When they were together some of Mollie's calm assurance rubbed off on her, giving her a confidence in herself that she usually lacked. Except for their slim figures, she and Mollie were a study in opposites. When they were together people often turned to look at them. Mollie's hair was as dark as Shay's was blond, as thick and heavy as Shay's was flyaway and wispy. And while Shay's hair was shoulder length, Mollie's hung just to her chin, so blunt cut that it looked as if she had whacked it off on a paper cutter. They had opposite tastes in clothes, too, Mollie usually dressing in primary colors, while Shay chose pastels.

"It's okay if I teamed us up with Sue and Beth, isn't it?" Mollie asked. "I mean . . ."

Shay smiled at her. "I'm sorry, but I can't make it to the D&D today, Mollie."

"Can't, or don't want to?"

Immediately Shay felt herself flushing. Subtlety had never been one of Mollie's traits. Mollie was sincere, but she was always as up-front as a hiccup. Sometimes Shay wondered if Mollie would ever make it as a psychologist. That was the long-range goal she talked about a lot. Could she really be subtle enough to guide others, guide rather than push? Shay sighed. At least she always knew where she stood with Mollie.

"Towe and I are going riding this afternoon, Mol. I mean, it's such a super day, and he said he had something special in mind."

"His class ring, maybe? Do you think he's going to ask you to wear his ring?"

She wished Mollie hadn't asked. Towe's silver class ring with its blue star sapphire set had been uppermost in Shay's thoughts ever since he had received it a few weeks ago. So far the ring had remained right on his finger.

"I haven't any idea what he has in mind, but I'll let you know after supper, okay?"

"I suppose." Mollie's shoulders slumped a bit and some of the enthusiasm drained from her voice. "But it seems like you never have time for your girlfriends anymore, Shay. Towe Williams always comes first with you."

Shawnee High School was on the edge of the city, and Shay looked into the distance at the blue-green Osage Hills on her left, at the gray skyscrapers of downtown Tulsa on her right. Mollie hadn't asked a question, so she made no reply. Lately her relationship with Towe had become a sore point with Mollie, and Mollie minced no words about it.

"I mean, you and Towe have spun a cocoon around yourselves that shuts everyone else out."

"I don't feel that way about us," Shay said, secretly liking Mollie's description of her relationship with Towe.

"Well, it's true," Mollie insisted.

Now Shay looked directly at Mollie. "I wish you'd try to understand, Mollie. Before I moved to Tulsa I never had a boyfriend. All last fall I never had a boyfriend and you were my only close girlfriend. But now it's really super to have Towe calling me, taking me out. I still can hardly believe I'm so lucky, and I don't want to blow it by being busy when he wants to be with me."

"But what about me? Don't I count?"

"Of course you count. You count a lot, Mollie. But it's different. I mean, if either of us cancels we can reschedule. A girl can't always do that with a boy."

"Yeah." Mollie kicked at a pebble. "You're right, but, well, I think you should think of the future."

"I *am* thinking of the future."

"I mean, how many girls end up married to the guy they dated during their junior year in high school?"

"Who said anything about marriage? I just want to know for sure that I have a date for Saturday night. That's as far in the future as I care to worry about."

"Well, you might as well face it. One of these days you and Towe are going to split up. Then where will you be if you don't have any girlfriends?"

Shay tried to keep her voice from sounding frosty. "Mind if I wait and worry about that big split when it happens?" Mollie meant well. She wouldn't be Mollie if she didn't say what she honestly thought. Why get uptight about something that wasn't going to happen? Both she and Towe were easygoing. Towe was a Pied Piper type, and she was quite willing to follow his lead.

"Mol, nobody has ever made me feel as special as Towe has. Having him as a steady is exciting. I'd think you'd be glad that I'm so happy."

"I am."

"You don't sound very glad."

"What do you expect me to say? That I'm delighted that you're bagging out on our Coke date? That I'm delighted to be going to the D&D with Beth and Sue, who laugh every time I mention becoming a psychologist? Lots of times I need you just to listen to me, Shay. Psychologists need a listening ear, too, you know."

"I'll listen to you tonight, okay? I'll call you right after supper."

"I'll sit by the phone." Mollie's words were sarcastic, but she smiled as they parted. Shay knew Mollie would never sit by the phone waiting for anyone to call. If only she had some of Mollie's confidence! Although Shay tried to hide it from the world, she was afraid of being alone, not just afraid of being dateless, but afraid of being out of it with the girls, too. She had felt so shunned, so different from these Oklahoma kids, when she first moved here from Connecticut that she never wanted to have to cope with those feelings again. Now when she looked into Towe's eyes she knew who she was. She was Towe's girl, and that was all that mattered.

With Towe at her side she could smile at the whole world. His friends had automatically become her friends. Thanks to Towe she had suddenly become one of the gang, not one of the small superelite in group, of course, but one of a nice large bunch of friendly kids.

Shay buttoned her jacket, surprised that the afternoon had turned so chilly, since it had been in the eighties almost all week. She lived only three blocks from school, and she hurried along the oak-lined sidewalk, looking up as a blue jay scolded from the light green of the spring foliage. But all the time she was thinking about Towe. What was the special thing he had in mind?

Turning onto the narrow sidewalk that led across the yard to her home, she admired the stone ranch-style house with its six Spanish arches across the wide front porch, its red-tiled roof. Two towering pecan trees on either side of the sidewalk shaded the house, and she smiled as she looked at the aluminum flanges that ringed the trees like stiff collars about eight feet from the ground. They were her father's makeshift invention, designed to keep squirrels from climbing the trees and stealing the nuts in the fall. How different all this was from the small apartment where she had lived in Westport. The populations of Oklahoma and Connecticut were almost the same, but Oklahoma allowed its citizens a lot more breathing space.

Shay hurried on inside and down a central hallway straight to her room. She hadn't expected her parents to be home. Her dad was a physical therapist at General Hospital, and her mother was a bookkeeper at the Frankoma Pottery plant just outside Tulsa. They didn't get off work until five.

After she had hung her jacket in her closet, she slipped into a pastel green sweatshirt that brought out her green eyes. She smiled to herself as she realized her whole room seemed designed to enhance her eyes. Dark green carpet. Soft green draperies and bedspread. Her dad had refinished her antique brass bed, and she and her mother had refinished the limed-oak dresser, chest of drawers, and study desk. She could feel comfortable in her room when she could feel comfortable nowhere else.

After pulling on her rough-cut riding boots, Shay hurried to the living room just in time to see Towe approaching. Even from a distance she could see a wrench protruding from his shirt pocket, and his jeans pockets looked lumpy, as if they were filled with nuts and bolts. Today Towe was riding a ten-speed, and she guessed his Pied Piper music was the rattle of spare auto parts in his pockets. She sighed. At least Towe had a goal in mind. He wanted to be an auto mechanic. Sometimes she envied both Mollie and Towe for being so sure of what they wanted to be and do. Her own future plans were very indefinite.

Now Towe turned into the driveway, and she smiled. She usually smiled whenever she saw Towe. Mollie had learned in psychology class that a person noticed another person's age, body build, and clothing before noticing anything else about that person, but Shay knew that Towe was the exception to that rule.

When people saw Towe the first thing they noticed was his flaming red hair. Or maybe they noticed his height first and then his hair. He was well over six feet tall and his hair drew the observer's eye up and up and up. That's what had earned him the nickname Towering Inferno, usually shortened to Towe. At first Shay had wondered if the nickname also referred to a hot temper, but it didn't. Towe was a live-and-let-live type. He liked everyone, and everyone liked him.

Shay opened the door before Towe knocked. "Hi! Ready to go?"

"You up to biking to the ranch?" Towe asked. "Got the carburetor out of my car so I can work on it tomorrow afternoon, but I could borrow Dad's wheels if you'd rather ride."

"Let's bike." Shay grinned up at him. "It won't take long." She watched the way his smile started at the left corner of his mouth, then spread across his lips, lighting his whole face.

Towe helped her wheel her ten-speed from the garage, and she smelled the faint scent of gasoline that usually clung to his work jeans.

"How's the car coming along?" she asked.

"Not too bad. Should have it in running condition by tomorrow night. Then on Sunday I'm going to overhaul the clutch."

"You really think you'll have it ready to sell by July?"

"I hope so. I'm counting on making about a thou on it, and that'll really help with my vo-tech tuition next fall."

They pedaled through the golden sunshine to the Redhill Ranch and Stable about a mile and a half beyond the city limits. Shay never tired of looking at the wide, rolling countryside where red earth showed through the early-spring growth of clover. In a field to her left, surrounded by buttercups and sunflowers, an old green-painted oil rig was slowly pumping, and on her right a newer orange-and-black rig stood at rest. Towe had explained that the rigs were set to pump only a certain number of minutes each hour. The pungent smell of oil hung in the air.

"Ever miss Connecticut?" Towe asked.

"Yeah, sometimes. Sometimes I miss being near New York City and shopping at Bloomie's, riding the subways, going to the Garden to a rock concert."

"Yeah, I'll bet you do miss all that."

"But owning my own registered quarter horse and being able to ride in the Saddle Club shows help make up for the other, Towe.'' And she wanted to say that he himself made Tulsa her favorite city. If her parents hadn't decided to move back to her dad's home state, she would never have met Towe Williams.

"What are you thinking?" Towe asked.

Shay felt heat rush to her face. "I was thinking how beautiful this ranch is, the white rail fence, the Appaloosas and quarter horses grazing in the pasture, the willows like green feather dusters growing along the creek."

"Some imagination." Towe smiled at her as they turned onto the dirt lane leading to the stable. "I've got a bit of Oklahoma Green Country to show you that I'll bet you've never seen before. Let's saddle up and get going. Thought we'd take Valley View Road. Not much traffic out that way."

Something she had never seen before, Shay thought, pumping harder to keep up with Towe's sudden burst of speed. A bit of Oklahoma didn't sound much like a class ring. She couldn't imagine what Towe had in mind. And Valley View Road! She had hoped they would just ride in the arena today. She needed to work Dancer in the ring if she expected her to be ready for her first show. She hid her disappointment. She could ride in the ring tomorrow morning, if not this afternoon.

They balanced their bicycles on their kickstands beside the tack-room door, grabbed lead ropes, and jogged to the pasture to catch their mounts. Her parents had bought Dancer for her last fall, and the mare had been bred to Shawnee Chief. She was to foal within a couple of months. Shay could hardly wait. Colt? Filly? She really didn't care, as long as both Dancer and the foal were okay. She planned to raise the foal, then sell it to help with expenses if she decided to go on to college.

She watched Dancer and King prick up their ears, then head toward them. A matched set. There wasn't a hand's difference in their height and they were both buckskins, both beauties with their sleek tan coats, their ebony manes and tails.

"Think you'll ever buy King?" Shay asked as the horses cantered toward them, responding to their whistles.

"I doubt it, Shay. I need all my money for school next fall, and as long as Mr. Harmon will let me ride in exchange for keeping his utility truck tuned up, I'll settle for that."

"I'm sure he's glad that King is getting some exercise," Shay said. "That's why he makes you such a special deal. Not many kids can ride whenever they please without owning their own horse." She snapped her lead rope onto Dancer's halter, patting her, inhaling the clean, sharp scent of horseflesh. "Shall we saddle up or ride bareback?"

"Your choice."

"Then let's saddle. I feel a lot more secure with a saddle under me."

Towe gave her a leg up, and they rode bareback to the stable, then saddled their mounts.

"Where to?" Shay leaned forward to pat Dancer's withers.

"Follow me." Towe reined King to the left, and they trotted the horses along the dirt lane to the gravel road south of the stable. They walked for another mile; then Towe turned onto a narrow, rutted path at their left.

"Where are you taking me?" Shay asked at last as the green undergrowth grew thick on both sides of the red dirt trail.

"I'm going to show you snowdrifts in May."

"You're kidding."

"No way. This is Blackberry Winter—at least, that's what the natives call it."

"Blackberry Winter? Never heard of it."

"Look." Towe lifted some branches of scrub oak aside and pointed to the hedgerow.

Shay gasped in surprise. Thousands of small white blossoms covered so many bushes growing in the thicket that they did indeed give the effect of snow.

"Blackberry bushes?" Shay asked.

"Right." Towe grinned at her.

"They're lovely!"

"Whenever we have a cold snap like this in May, nature lovers know that the wild blackberries are in bloom."

"Blackberry Winter," Shay murmured. "It's really picturesque."

"Guess it's the counterpart of October's Indian summer. I thought you'd enjoy seeing it."

"Can we dismount and smell the blossoms?" Shay felt very special to think that Towe had taken the time to show her the wild blackberries. She wished she had brought a camera. What a picture she could have taken, the white froth of blossoms as a backdrop for the two buckskins and for Towe and his red hair. She tried to memorize the scene so she would remember it always.

"I don't think you'd really like getting close enough to smell the blossoms," Towe said. "No way. There are thorns. Scads of them. It's not worth the pain."

Shay hid her disappointment. "Then let's just enjoy them from a distance." She waited for Towe to pull King alongside Dancer, to take her hand as he sometimes did.

Maybe he wanted to give her his class ring in this lovely setting. She waited expectantly, but Towe remained where he was, slightly behind her, and after a few moments she turned Dancer and they headed back toward the stable. They rode without speaking, and the only sounds were the gentle squeak of leather, the quiet snuffling of the horses, the muted thumping of hoofs against the soft dirt.

"Want to work out in the ring for a while?" Shay asked as they came to the arena gate. "We've got another hour or so yet."

"You go ahead, Shay." Towe glanced at his watch. "I promised Dad I'd wash and wax the family car this afternoon, so I'd better get on with it."

Shay sat very still on Dancer's back, sensing that something was the matter, yet not quite knowing what it was. Why was Towe acting so strangely? He had never ended one of their riding sessions early before. Had he been disappointed in her reaction to the blackberry blossoms? Had he been afraid she wouldn't want to wear his ring? Or did riding in the arena bore him?

"If you don't want to work the horses in the arena, we can just ride around the pasture down by the creek," she offered.

Towe glanced at his watch again. "I'd really like to, Shay. But not today."

"I'm sorry you have to go." Shay hesitated. "Maybe I should wrap it up, too."

"Oh, you don't need to do that. Go ahead and work Dancer. I know how important winning a trophy in that show is to you. My sister was high-point winner one summer, and I can remember how excited she was about getting to represent the Saddle Club at the state fair. It's worth trying for. Hang in there.''

''Well, okay, if you're sure you don't care. We'll ride again tomorrow morning, won't we?''

''Sure thing,'' Towe said. ''I'll get up early and work on my car, then pick you up.''

Shay waited while Towe unsaddled King, brushed him down, and turned him back into the pasture; then she waved to him as he mounted his bike and pedaled toward town. Why did she feel so deserted? She had worked Dancer alone a lot of times. Lots of times she was the only one at the stable. The big rush of people usually came on Saturday and Sunday afternoons.

She urged Dancer into the ring.

''Walk,'' she commanded. She felt the late-afternoon sun warm her head and shoulders as they walked around the ring.

''Trot,'' she signaled with voice and knees. Dancer had a trot so smooth Shay felt she might have been sitting in a rocking chair. She smiled. A smooth trot always impressed the judges.

''Canter.'' Dancer took off at a lope, but Shay reined her to a quick stop, smelling dust rise in the air, feeling it grit in her mouth. She walked the mare a short distance, trotted her a few seconds, then repeated the command to canter. This time Dancer took the correct lead and they circled the ring at a canter, then reversed without breaking pace.

''Enough for today,'' Shay said as she walked Dancer toward the hickory hitching rail and dismounted. She tied the mare to the rail before she went to the tack room for the currycomb and a hoof pick. She always treated

Dancer to a thorough grooming before turning her out to pasture.

When she had finished brushing and combing the mare's coat and cleaning her feet, she stood back to admire her, wondering again just when the foal would be born. Dr. Richards said a while yet, but sometimes it was hard for a vet to tell. It could be sooner than that. Or later.

Shay led Dancer to the pasture, opening and closing the gate carefully; then she watched the mare trot toward the creek with mane and tail flying like black flags in the wind. She was a beauty. How could any judge resist her?

The sun was dropping low in the sky by the time Shay got home, and the minute she went inside, her mother sent her to the drugstore to pick up a paperback book she had ordered. Shay was glad to run the errand. It would be one less thing she had to do tomorrow when she was eager to get back to the ranch.

Sneed's Drugs was at the intersection of Main Street and First Street, across from the D&D, and Shay was inside and waiting for Mr. Sneed to wrap the book for her when she glanced out the window and saw Towe. He was leaving the D&D with Chip Parris, Mollie's sometimes boyfriend, and three other boys from the senior class. She stepped behind a rack of paperbacks quickly, not wanting Towe to look across the street and know she had seen him.

Her hands were moist as she paid Mr. Sneed for the book. She pretended to study the magazines for a few minutes before she left the store, and then she looked cautiously both ways before she stepped into the street. What had Towe been doing at the D&D with the guys?

Had he decided not to do the wash-and-wax job on the family car?

She hurried down the street, eager for the security of her own home. There could be a hundred reasons why Towe had decided not to work on the car, yet she couldn't help wondering about it.

2

Shay hurried home, pausing just inside the front entry-way for a moment to watch the way the late-afternoon sun was shining through the colored glass in the fanlight above the oak door. Did all the colors seem tinged with blue, or was it just her mood? She brushed her bangs from her eyes and went on to the kitchen, laying the paperback on the countertop where her mother would be sure to see it. She could hear her walking about in the basement laundry room.

"Mom, I'm home."

"Good, dear. Be up in a minute."

Using a hotpad, Shay lifted the lid on the crock-pot. She and her mother and father took turns preparing dinner, and today was her turn. She had done most of the work that morning before she went to school, chopping meat, peeling onions, potatoes, carrots. She inhaled the enticing aroma of the stew, replaced the lid, unplugged the pot. By the time she had made a green salad and popped half a loaf of buttered French bread into the oven, her mother arrived to help set the table. When just the three of them were present, they always ate at the small drop-leaf table in the kitchen.

"Smells good, Shay," her mother said.

"Smells *great*," her dad said, stepping through the back doorway from the garage just in time to overhear his wife's words.

"Thanks." Shay tilted her cheek for her dad's kiss as she carried the crock-pot to the table. For a moment her dad stood with his arm around his wife, and Shay noticed how much alike the two of them looked. They were even dressed alike in tan slacks and white shirts. Of course her father was taller than her mother, but they both had the same slim, wiry build, the same light brown hair and blue eyes, the same high cheekbones. She wondered if people who lived together for twenty years just automatically grew to look alike. What would have happened if one of them had been born with wispy blond hair and the other with flaming red hair?

"Are we ready to eat?" her dad asked.

"Yes," Shay said. "Just as soon as you sit down."

"Give me time to change into some comfortable clothes." Her dad headed down the hallway toward the bedrooms.

Shay looked at the clock. Six-thirty. Back in Connecticut they had never eaten dinner before seven-thirty, but that schedule hadn't worked out here. They had really been surprised one night soon after they had moved in when well-meaning neighbors dropped by at seven to welcome them to the block, not realizing she and her parents hadn't eaten dinner. The two families got to talking, and the neighbors stayed for almost two hours. She had about fainted from hunger. It had been her mother's night to cook dinner, and there had been no way she could stretch three chops and three potatoes to serve five people. Anyway, the callers had already eaten their dinner. That fact had come up casually in the conversation.

"Hurry up, Henry," her mother called. "Shay probably has plans for the evening." Then, looking at Shay, she asked, "What are you and Towe doing tonight?"

Shay turned her back to her mother as she put the bread in a serving basket and covered it. "Nothing, Mom. But I'm going to call Mollie."

"Oh, I just assumed . . ."

"Towe and I went riding this afternoon, and Mollie and I have plans tonight. Mollie thinks I've been neglecting her." Why had she thought her mother wouldn't notice Towe's absence? Ever since Christmas she and Towe had been going out on Friday night, Saturday night, and Sunday afternoon. But this was the second Friday Towe hadn't made plans.

Her father returned to the kitchen wearing cords, a plaid shirt, and loafers, and they sat down to eat. She spooned stew onto her plate and pretended to listen to her parents' small talk about their day's activities, but her mind was on Towe. Had she done something to hurt his feelings? She tried to think back. Sometimes they argued a bit about what they would do on the weekends, but there had been no such arguments lately. On Wednesday after school she had gone to Towe's house to watch him work on his car. And this afternoon everything had seemed fine between them until Towe had left early.

"You're awfully quiet, Shay," her father said. "Something bothering you?"

"No, Dad. Everything's fine."

"Guess we all get spring fever this time of the year." He went on eating his stew.

"Mighty good dinner, Shay," her mother said.

"Thanks, Mom."

"Shay," her dad said, "do you know an Eric Chapin?"

Shay looked at her father, trying to think. "No, I don't believe I do. Why?"

"His parents brought him to the emergency room late this afternoon, brought him in from Redhill Stable. Sprained ankle. They were afraid it might be broken, but it wasn't. Just thought you might know him."

"Was he tall and thin, with dark brown hair and green eyes?" Shay asked.

Her dad grinned at her. "For not knowing the boy, you give a very good description."

Shay wrinkled her nose at her father. "Well, I *have* seen a new boy at the stable once or twice, and I've seen him at school, too, but I haven't met him or anything. He must be the one. Too bad about the ankle."

"Does he ride?" her mother asked.

"I really don't know, Mom. I've seen him grooming an Appaloosa, but I haven't seen him riding."

Shay was glad when the meal ended, when the small talk stopped and her parents went to the living room to read the paper and watch TV. She cleaned up the kitchen, then hurried to her room. Pulling the hall telephone and its long cord through her doorway, she sat down on the edge of her bed and dialed Mollie.

"Thought you'd never call," Mollie said.

"We just finished eating."

"I thought maybe you'd forgotten. And a person doesn't forget things . . ."

". . . things she really wants to remember." Shay finished the sentence. "Don't psych me out tonight, Mol. Let's get together and see if we can psych out Towe."

"He giving you a bad time or something?"

"I'm not sure."

"Give. Doc McNamara can't help you unless you let her have all the details."

"Over the phone?"

"Why not?"

"I thought maybe we could meet at the D&D and talk."

"No way. I don't want everyone in school to know I don't have a date on Friday night. If I keep a low profile, maybe kids will think I'm out with some handsome guy that I'm keeping top secret."

"Good psychology." Shay laughed in spite of herself. "Maybe we could talk at the public library. None of our crowd would be caught dead in *there* on a weekend night."

"Okay, later. What's the problem? Tell me now so I can be thinking about it."

"It's sort of strange." Shay hesitated.

"Shay, just spit it out, will you? Tell it like it is, and maybe I can help."

"Okay. Okay." Shay sat up straighter. She could be as up-front as Mollie, couldn't she? And Mollie wouldn't tell a soul. She said that learning to keep your mouth shut was a top requirement for psychologists.

"Shay, are you still there?"

"Mollie, Towe bagged out early on our riding session this afternoon. Said he had to wax the family car." She blurted the words, then realized how silly they must sound to Mollie.

"So?"

"Less than an hour later I saw him at the D&D with a bunch of guys." The line hummed for a moment.

"And you think he was putting you on about having to wax the car?"

"What else can I think?"

"Maybe his dad suddenly needed the car and Towe couldn't work on it. Or maybe he broke out and suddenly learned he was allergic to wax. Or maybe the guys had a problem that only Towe could solve. Jeepers."

"Or maybe he's losing interest in me, Mollie. Do you know something you haven't told me?"

"Like what?"

"I don't know what, but just this afternoon you were talking about Towe and me splitting up."

"That was just a coincidence, but, Shay, worse things have happened than a guy and a girl losing interest in each other."

"Mol! With a friend like you, who needs enemies?"

"What do you expect me to say? You know I don't believe in going steady."

"But I do! And I'm the one with the problem."

"Maybe you're just making a problem. Don't borrow trouble. Anyway, there *are* worse things than spending a Saturday night with the girls now and then. Why don't I pick you up in about a half hour and we'll really talk?"

"Okay, Mollie. See you then."

Shay returned the telephone to its niche in the hall and sat down to think. Of course Mollie was right. She might be borrowing trouble. Maybe she shouldn't have said anything to Mollie at all. Suddenly she was very homesick for Connecticut and the friends she had left there. The girlfriends. She hadn't had a boyfriend.

Maybe that was part of her problem. She didn't quite know how to deal with boys. She had entered Shawnee High a month after school had started last fall. Cliques of girls were already firmly established, and she hadn't seemed to fit into any of them. Nobody had been really friendly to her except Mollie—and Towe. Now she knew that Mollie was pretty much of a free spirit where the cliques were concerned, and besides that Mollie had been analyzing her. It wasn't every day Mollie had a new and unsuspecting personality to work on. But Shay didn't resent Mollie's attitude. It had been a lucky situation for both of them, because they had become close friends.

But it had been Towe who had really made her forget old ties back east and begin relating to the here and now. A senior. President of his class. Towe was a guy who had earned popularity without being a football hero or a basketball star, a guy who had a lot of junior and senior girls hanging after him. But he had chosen Shay. How nice it was to have been chosen.

When Towe had asked her to go steady just before Christmas, she had accepted, knowing she had never been so happy in all her life. And once the kids knew she was Towe's girl, they looked at her with new respect. She had been asked to join the Pep Club, and she and Towe were always invited to lots of parties.

What would happen to her if Towe vanished from her life? She couldn't bear being a nobody again. How would she ever be able to cope? She needed Towe. Without him she felt like nothing. She glanced at her

28

watch and stood, reaching for her jacket. She was glad she had told Mollie what had happened. Maybe Mollie was right. Maybe there wasn't a problem, at least not yet. And if there was one in the offing, maybe Mollie could help her figure out a way to avoid it.

Shay stood by the front door until Mollie honked for her; then she told her parents goodbye and hurried outside. "Be back early," she called over her shoulder.

The night was brisk and chilly, but there was an early-evening moon, orange, big as a pumpkin, lighting the pecan trees, the lawn. In the mellow glow she could see that Mollie had someone with her in the car. As Shay approached, a boy alighted and held the door for her.

"I'm Randy Russell," he said. "Mollie's cousin. She's stuck with me for the evening." He motioned to the front seat. "Hop in. Mollie's promised to show me the bright lights of Tulsa."

Shay suddenly felt like a punctured tire. With a third person along, she and Mollie weren't going to be able to talk. At least, they couldn't discuss anything personal or private. Why hadn't Mollie warned her they wouldn't be alone?

"It's nice to meet you, Randy." Shay scooted onto the seat, easing close to Mollie, and Randy slid in beside her. Tall. Muscular. He seemed a couple of years older than they were. Or was it just his clothes that made him seem older? He was wearing brown cord slacks and a brown turtleneck shirt under a tweed jacket with leather elbow patches. Randy's hair was flying every which way all over his head.

"Thought we'd go to the D&D for a malt, Shay," Mollie said. "Okay?"

"Sure. Sounds great." What had happened to the

public library? she wondered. "But I just finished eating, so I may have to settle for a short Coke."

Mollie parked the car near the D&D, and Randy walked between them as they crossed the street and approached the teen hangout. A red neon sign reading Dari-Delite blinked on and off above the door, and Shay held on to a black hand railing as she climbed the three steps to the entry. Even before she stepped inside she smelled the enticing fragrance of chocolate and peppermint.

The interior of the dairy bar was brightly lighted toward the front, and customers could sit on red plastic stools at the horseshoe-shaped bar while they sipped soft drinks or waited for Mr. Rogers to hand-pack their ice-cream order. Booths on either side of the bar were more dimly lighted, and on toward the back of the establishment a large dancing area and a jukebox attracted dancers of various ages.

"Years ago this place used to be a bowling alley," Mollie explained to Randy. "That's why it's so long and narrow."

"I would never have guessed," he said, grinning.

Mollie led the way to a booth, slid in first, and motioned for Shay to sit beside her. "We'll let you sit across from us, Randy. That way, when the after-the-movie crowd arrives, the kids won't know which one of us is with the handsome stranger."

"Flattery will get you everywhere, cuz. How about a double malted?"

While a waitress took their orders Shay studied Randy Russell. His hair was dark like Mollie's, and although it did look wildly tousled, there was a casualness about it that was becoming to him. It suited his offhand manner, his easy smile. His eyes were like dark half-spheres of polished amber, and they seemed more mature than the rest of his face as they looked at the world with a seriousness that belied his light banter. She thought about Mollie's words: *The kids won't know which of us is with the handsome stranger.*

Was this Mollie's idea of a way to make boys notice her? Or was it her way of trying to make Towe just a bit jealous? What if Towe came in with another girl? No. He wouldn't do that. She and Towe were steadies. They wouldn't cheat on each other. She didn't expect to see Towe in here tonight, but she knew there would be plenty of kids who would relay the word to him that she had been here. She wasn't sure she liked Mollie's plan, whatever it was.

"Randy dropped in right after you phoned, Shay. I would have called you back, but I didn't think you'd mind if he joined us."

"Of course not." Shay smiled at him.

"Mollie tells me you're interested in horses and riding," Randy said, looking directly at Shay.

"Yes. I used to ride back east, but western riding is a lot different. I almost had to learn over again."

"Shay's going to show her horse in the Saddle Club events this spring and summer," Mollie said. "And as trophy queen she'll represent the club at the state fair in the fall."

"Mollie!" Shay scowled, then looked at Randy. "That's my dream, but it's not a certainty."

"A person has to dream before anything will happen, right?" He grinned at her.

"I suppose so." She surprised herself. Being able to talk to strangers was usually not her thing, but Randy was so relaxed it made her able to relax, too. "Where do you go to school?"

"I'm a sophomore at Oklahoma A&M. And I've got a few dreams, too. One of them is to be admitted to veterinary school. And another is to write a book. And a third is to go into business of some sort, a business related to animals, maybe."

"Really?" Shay asked. "Then you must be a real animal lover."

"Right. Especially horses. I'd like to see yours."

"It's a registered quarter horse. A buckskin. Black mane and tail. Tiger stripes on the inside of the legs."

"Maybe you could go out to the stable and see it tomorrow," Mollie said.

Randy shook his head. "Can't make it. Have to meet a tour group at Tulsa U. But maybe another time."

"Maybe you'll be another James Herriot," Mollie said. "Maybe you'll write a book about animals."

"*All Things Sick and Sorrowful*," Randy said. "How's that for a title?"

"Terrible," Mollie said. Then she paused, glancing at the door. "Hey, look who just came in. Ginger Netherton."

"Who's she?" Randy asked.

"Ginger's the glamor girl of Shawnee High," Mollie said.

Shay noted Ginger's designer jeans, her copper-colored shirt and shoes that just matched her copper-colored hair, but most of all she noted that Ginger was headed toward them although she seldom bothered to speak to either of them at school.

"Hi, gang," Ginger said, letting her gaze linger on Randy. "What's new?"

Shay smelled the heavy perfume that wafted from Ginger's hair and clothes.

"If you mean who's new, this is Randy Russell," Mollie said. "He's here for a meeting at Tulsa U."

"Oh, a college man." Ginger fluttered her eyelashes at Randy. "What are you studying?"

"Prevet medicine," Randy said.

"Very nice," Ginger said. "If I had a sick horse, you'd be the very first person I'd call."

That's our Ginger, Shay thought. She can deliver an insult to a guy in a way that makes him like it—like it and remember her name.

"Want to join us?" Randy asked.

Shay tried not to groan.

"Sorry." Ginger smiled at Randy. "No can do tonight, but I'm in the book. Call me sometime." Ginger smiled again, then hurried to join a group on the dance floor.

"Stop staring," Mollie said, glaring at Randy. "I think I may be sick."

Shay brushed her bangs back and said nothing, mildly irritated that Mollie hadn't made it clear to Ginger that Randy was her cousin. But what did it matter? If Mollie wanted to pretend Randy was her date, that was her business, but it really wasn't Mollie's usual way of doing things.

Shay was surprised at how quickly the evening passed. The three of them talked of horses, horse shows, the psychology of making a horse obey.

It wasn't until she was back at home that Shay realized she hadn't worried about Towe at all. Of course, she hadn't talked to Mollie about personal matters in front of Randy. And maybe it was just as well that she and Mollie hadn't spent the evening rapping about Towe and a problem that might not exist.

She was going riding with Towe tomorrow morning, wasn't she? If anything had been wrong between them, he would have canceled out. She felt irritated at herself for not having more faith in him. If Towe said he had to wax a car, then he had to wax a car. And there was some logical explanation for his being at the D&D with the guys.

3

On Saturday morning Shay rose early in order to do her household chores before Towe picked her up to go to the stable. She dressed in old jeans, a red-and-white gingham shirt, and old sneakers. Plenty of time to pull on her riding boots later.

She gathered the soiled bedding and towels and placed them in the machine to wash while she dusted her room and vacuumed the carpet. By the time she had finished those jobs, the linens were ready to be transferred from washer to dryer.

"Let's hang them out today," her mother said as Shay began loading the dryer. "It's such a pretty, warm day. And I love the scent of line-dried sheets."

"Okay, Mom." Shay smiled. Today she and her mother were almost look-alikes. Her mother frequently wore jeans around the house on Saturday, and today, although she wore a blue chambray shirt, she had a red-and-white gingham scarf tied around her hair.

Shay hoped hanging the sheets wouldn't make her late getting to the stable. She glanced at her watch. Dr.

Richards was supposed to check Dancer this morning, and Shay wanted to be there to hear what he had to say.

"I'll help you," her mother said. "Towe's stopping at nine, right?"

"Right. But I've got plenty of time."

"I'll help you, anyway. I need an excuse to be outside, and I like having a chance to talk to you once in a while. Seems we never have time to really sit down and talk."

"Not too much to talk about," Shay said, knowing her mother wouldn't understand her worries about Towe. She really didn't understand them herself, and she had vowed to put them from her mind.

"Things going okay for you at school?" her mother asked.

It was a standard question; she gave a standard answer. "Fine. Won't be long until school's out. Just a few more weeks."

"What do you plan to do this summer?" Her mother picked up the clothes basket and started upstairs.

Shay grabbed the bag of clothespins. "I'd like to get a job of some kind."

"Like what?"

"I don't know. Maybe something at the stable." She followed her mother into the backyard. "Mr. Harmon needs teachers, and he needs someone to exercise horses when people go on vacation. Also, I thought I might talk to Dr. Richards."

"The vet?"

"Uh-huh. Sometimes veterinaries let a person who is interested in becoming a veterinarian go along with them on their rounds to observe and help out, under supervision, of course."

"Shay!" her mother exclaimed, setting the clothes basket down and looking directly at her. "I didn't know you were thinking about becoming a veterinarian."

Shay felt herself blushing. She hadn't known it, either, until the words just popped out. "Well, I thought I might be interested. I really like animals." She picked up a sheet and began pinning it to the line.

"What gave you the idea?" her mother asked.

Shay laughed, thinking that it really wasn't so hard to talk with her mother at times. "It's crazy, Mom, but last night Mollie had this cousin with her, and he's in prevet medicine at A&M. I guess he gave me the idea. He seemed so sincere and so eager to be a vet. But maybe it's not a thing for girls."

"Almost any occupation's a thing for girls these days. It sounds like a good idea to look into the possibilities, the requirements. Tell me about this cousin. What was he like?"

"Neat. A very neat guy." Shay shook the wrinkles from a pillowcase and hung it next to the sheet.

"That tells me a whole lot." Her mother laughed. "But I won't pry. It's good for a girl to have a few secrets about her boyfriends."

"Gol, Mom. Randy isn't a boyfriend. He's just Mollie's cousin who was passing through town."

"Maybe he'll pass through town again sometime."

They finished hanging the clothes and went back inside. Shay was sorry she had mentioned Randy Russell. She knew her mother wasn't really strong for her going steady with Towe, although she had never forbidden it. But she didn't want to do or say anything that would make her mother think she was going to start dating other boys. How had Randy's name slipped into their conversation? Oh, yeah, vet school. She would make it clear to her mother that her interest in Randy was only professional.

It was past nine when Shay returned to her room after hanging the clothes. She scowled. It wasn't like Towe to be late. If anything, he was usually ahead of time. Maybe her clock was fast. She hurried to the living room to check the time on the TV clock. Nine-ten. She went back to her room to change clothes. She hadn't planned to change clothes, but it took up a few minutes. She put on newer jeans, a blue-and-green plaid shirt, a fringed leather vest. And she tugged on her riding boots.

Nine-twenty. Still no Towe. She paced the hallway, eyeing the telephone. She could call him, remind him. No. She wasn't about to do that. But maybe she should. Maybe someone who had seen her at the D&D last night had already told Towe she had been there, and with another boy. Lots of kids had seen her. Someone might have jumped to conclusions. Maybe she owed Towe an explanation. She reached for the phone just as it rang. She jumped, but then relief flooded through her. She was glad she had let Towe call her instead of calling him.

"What's up, Shay?"

For a moment Shay couldn't answer, she was so surprised to hear Mollie's voice. She had been so sure it was going to be Towe on the other end of the line.

"Hi, Mollie. Nothing's up. Why do you ask?"

"Because you said you had a nine o'clock date with Towe, and it's nine-thirty now. I was calling to talk with your mother about buying tickets to summer theater."

"I'll call her."

"No. Wait. What's with you and Towe?"

"He hasn't shown up yet. He must have been delayed."

"And you're just sitting there? Just sitting there waiting around for him?"

"Well, yes, I was waiting to see if something had . . . had happened to him."

"Happened to him! What do you think might have happened? Shay, waiting around is the worst thing in the world you could do. For Pete's sake, pull your socks up and get with it."

"What's that supposed to mean?"

"I mean, first Towe bags out on a riding date early, and now he stands you up. You can't afford to let him get by with it."

"I don't know for sure that he's stood me up," Shay said. "Maybe something has happened, something he can't help. An emergency."

"Yeah, sure. I suppose he lost his voice, and I suppose his phone went dead. Shay, you can't just sit around there waiting for him to show up. How about me going out to the stable with you?"

"Well, I don't know."

"I'll pick you up in five minutes. I've got the car. See ya."

The connection went dead before Shay could reply, and she stared at the receiver for a moment before she replaced it in its cradle. Mollie was so pushy sometimes. Well, it would serve her right to get over here just as Towe arrived. She would just have to realize that three was a crowd and go on home. Or maybe she could go riding with them just this once if Towe didn't mind.

But when Mollie arrived, Towe was still absent. And it was past nine-thirty.

"Let's go, Shay. Move it."

"Got to tell Mom I'm leaving." Shay turned and called to her mother, who came into the kitchen, dustcloth in hand.

"Oh, hello, Mollie," Mrs. Stuart said. "How nice of you to drive Shay to the stable."

"Tell Towe I've left," Shay said. "Tell him I waited a half hour, then decided to go on."

"Hey, Mrs. Stuart," Mollie interrupted, "don't tell him *that*. Tell him she left at 9:01."

"You girls!" Shay's mother laughed. "Go on with you. Have a good time. It's too nice a day to stay indoors waiting for anyone."

They rode to the stable, with Shay listening to Mollie lecture her on having self-respect; but after she stopped the car, Mollie apologized. "I'm sorry, Shay. It's really none of my business, is it?"

"Don't be sorry for me. I don't want your pity."

"I mean, I'm sorry that you're so uptight about Towe. No guy is worth it. Believe me, if Chip stood me up, even once, I'd never go out with him again."

Shay refrained from reminding Mollie that Chip seldom called her as it was. Their dating was really a casual thing, a once-a-month thing, if Mollie was lucky.

"You want to ride today, Mollie? You can ride Dancer if you want to. Mr. Harmon likes me to exercise Whirlwind for him when I have time. I want to work Dancer in the ring, but there will be plenty of time for that, too, after we ride together."

"I'll just watch today, okay? You put Dancer through her paces, and I'll play judge and tell you when she goes into a wrong lead or something."

"I can tell when she goes into a wrong lead, but you

could call the signals for me the way the announcer does at a real show. Sometimes when I call them myself I make it easy for her to take the correct lead.''

''Deal!'' Mollie parked her car away from the stable, and they walked to the aluminum pasture gate. Shay could see Dancer grazing on tender green grass at the far corner of the field where willows shaded a rushing stream. She whistled and waited. Dancer lifted her head with ears pricked forward; then she trotted toward them.

''You've really got her trained to come on signal,'' Mollie said. ''That's one reason I gave up riding. Hated chasing the horse all over the pasture. By the time I caught it, the riding time would be half gone.''

Shay laughed, and she was so intent on watching Dancer's graceful gait as she approached that she didn't notice the boy at her side until he spoke.

''Are you Shay Stuart?''

Shay turned to face him. Eric Chapin. She knew without being told. He was tall; even hunched on the crutches, he was tall. And muscular. His brown knit shirt revealed rippling muscles underneath. He had dark hair the mellow brown color of old oak leaves, and his features were cameo sharp. Shay remembered seeing him in the halls at school, remembered him better than she had let on to her dad. The new boy. At first all the girls had been excited over him; then the word got around that Eric was aloof and stuck-up. She felt on guard as she answered him.

''Yes, I'm Shay Stuart.''

''Got a message for you,'' Eric said.

Shay could feel her heart racing. So Towe had called the stable. He hadn't expected her to wait for him and he had tried to get in touch.

"Dr. Richards called," Eric said. "He asked me to tell you he can't make it here to check your mare today."

"Why not?" Did she feel let down because the message hadn't been from Towe, or because the vet wasn't going to show?

Eric shrugged. "Don't know the why of it. That's just the message he asked me to deliver. Is your mare sick?" He peered at Dancer, who had now reached the fence and was contentedly munching grass. "She looks healthy enough."

"She's supposed to foal soon," Shay said, "but I think she's okay. Are you Eric Chapin?"

Now the boy blushed, looking as if he might turn and leave. Then he seemed to regroup and decide to stay. "Yes, I am. How did you know my name?"

"You saw my dad yesterday at the hospital. The physical therapist."

"Mr. Stuart." The boy grinned. "I remember him. He and the doctor really gave me the word about what to do and not to do while this dumb ankle heals."

"How did you hurt it?" Mollie asked, eyeing his crutches and his wrapped foot.

"Fell off my horse." Now his face turned a dull red. "Got clumsy."

"Sometimes that happens." Shay smiled, trying to make Eric feel more at ease. This boy wasn't aloof and stuck-up. He was shy, just as she had been last fall. What a switch. She was the one who usually had a king-size case of the shys.

"Yeah, well. Anyway, I won't be riding for a while. Got to use these crutches for at least two weeks and maybe longer."

"It must be a bad sprain."

"Yeah."

"Well, thanks for delivering the message from Dr. Richards."

"You're welcome." Eric turned and began swinging himself toward the stable on the crutches.

"Poor guy," Shay said. "I'll bet he was planning to ride in that first show. I know how he must be feeling."

"Do you know him?" Mollie asked.

"No. I've just seem him around the stable grooming his horse. He's got a good-looking Appaloosa."

"He must get along with horses better than he gets along with people," Mollie said. "Wish I had time to psych him out."

Shay ran to the pasture gate, opened it, and gripped Dancer's halter, leading her to the hitching rail. From the corner of her eye she saw Eric at another hitching rail, trying to coax his horse into position for grooming. But the Appaloosa wasn't used to seeing him on the crutches, and every time Eric got near him, the horse shied.

"Why don't you saddle Dancer and ride her around the pasture, Mollie?" Shay asked. "I'll help Eric with his horse for a minute."

"You'll probably scare him into the next county. Eric, I mean, not the horse. I think he's one shy guy."

"I'll take my chances. He was nice enough to give me the vet's message, and he *is* having trouble." She brought her saddle and bridle from the tack room and gave them to Mollie; then she approached Eric slowly, trying not to frighten either him or his horse.

"Maybe I can help," Shay said.

"He's usually not this way." Eric's face flushed again.

"He's frightened of the crutches," Shay said. "Horses are supposed to be smart, but sometimes they can be pretty dumb. Why don't you sit down, lay the crutches behind you, and let me try coaxing him to the hitching rail?"

Eric hesitated a second, then nodded and handed her the lead rope. "Okay. Give it a try. But be careful. He's not too fond of strangers."

"What's his name?"

"Cherokee."

Shay turned and approached the gelding slowly and cautiously, but with confidence, thinking how crazy it was she could deal with a thousand pounds of horseflesh, yet she couldn't deal with a hundred seventy-five pounds of Towe Williams. But never mind that. Cherokee stood steady, and when she reached him, she lifted her hand slowly, then snapped the lead rope in place quickly. In the next moment the gelding was tethered to the hitching rail.

"Say, you're okay," Eric said. "I really didn't think you could do it."

"I have a way with horses," Shay said, then immediately regretted the words. She didn't want this guy to think she was a bragger. "I mean, horses usually respond to me."

"Yeah, I know what you mean." Now Eric stood again, but when he picked up his crutches, Cherokee tried to rear, stamping and pawing the earth, turning his head against the restriction of the lead rope.

"I've got an idea," Shay said.

"I'm listening." Eric grinned at her.

"You're going to have to be careful, Eric. Did your doctor really say you could ride?"

44

"No, he didn't. But I wasn't going to try to ride. I was just going to see if I could groom Cherokee. He's used to having a going-over with the currycomb every day."

"Well, he's going to have to get used to seeing you on crutches first." Shay walked to Eric. "Can you manage on just one crutch for a minute?"

"I suppose so."

She took one of his crutches. "I'm going to let him see it. Let him smell it. That's the way I broke Dancer to the saddle. Slow and easy at first. Once she got used to seeing the saddle and smelling it, there was no problem."

"I should have thought of that myself," Eric said. "That's the same way I trained Cherokee. Never thought about him being scared of the crutches. But go ahead. Just be careful."

Shay carried the crutch in front of her, then stood still several feet away from Cherokee. His eyes rolled wildly, but he held steady. She approached him a step at a time. When he accepted her presence directly in front of him, she lifted the crutch and held it to his nose as she reached to pat him, crooning in his ear.

"Steady boy, steady. This won't hurt a bit. Steady, boy."

The gelding stretched his neck, sniffing the crutch, and in a few minutes his eyes stopped rolling. He lowered his head. Shay leaned the crutch against the hitching rail where he could see it and smell it some more; then she turned to Eric.

"Your horse. Don't think you'll have any trouble getting him to stand still for a grooming now."

"Hey, thanks, Shay. Thanks a bunch."

Shay left Eric and Cherokee, standing by the fence until Mollie rode up on Dancer.

"You've done a great job of training her, Shay. She has a way of going that's really okay."

"Hope the judges think so." Shay mounted as soon as Mollie's feet hit the ground. "Let me take her around the pasture once; then I think I'd better let her rest until I find out what the vet has to say. I wouldn't want to do anything to put her or the foal in danger."

"Is she having problems?" Mollie asked.

"Not that I know of, but I want to be sure everything's okay."

"Yeah. You're right."

Shay watched Mollie stroll back to the car; then she headed Dancer toward the creek at a walk. She could feel Eric's gaze on her back as she signaled Dancer to trot. Was Eric impressed? But why did she care? Eric Chapin wasn't a judge. It was the show judges she needed to impress.

Walk. Trot. Canter. Shay worked Dancer for about twenty minutes. Sometimes the mare was perfection in these practice sessions. If only she would perform as well under show conditions! Would she get rattled at the music that would be blaring over the loudspeaker, at the other horses in the ring, at the general confusion?

Before Shay owned Dancer she had watched some shows last fall. The events had fascinated her. Pony Lead-in and Walk-Trot for the little kids. Western Pleasure for juniors and adults. Pole Bending. Barrel Racing. Tandem Bareback. Jumping. She had watched all the events carefully and she had decided to concentrate on doing her very best at Western Pleasure. The gaits required for that event were gaits she could use in everyday trail riding with Towe or Mollie.

"Hey!" Mollie called to her, jogging toward the fence. "It's almost noon. I've got to get home. You about ready to go?"

"Be right with you." Shay headed for the hitching rail, where she tethered Dancer. Eric was nowhere in sight, and his Appaloosa was grazing in the south pasture with the rest of the horses. Shay unsaddled Dancer, then stepped into the tack room, inhaling the scent of leather and saddle soap as she stored her tack in the space assigned to her. Back outside she gave Dancer a quick grooming, led her to the pasture, then joined Mollie in the car.

"What's your hurry, Mol?"

"Got to help Dad with some book work this afternoon." Mollie laughed. "I think he's grooming me to be a cattle rancher just in case the psychology business isn't all that great."

"What do you have to do?"

"Record feed bills, grain storage bills, that sort of thing. I hate working with numbers, but at least Dad lets me use a pocket calculator."

"Guess it doesn't hurt to know about the business side of things," Shay said. "But I'm glad all I have to do is help Mom in the garden. She's determined that we're going to eat homegrown veggies this summer."

Mollie let Shay out at her house, and the minute she stepped inside, her mother called to her.

"Towe phoned you, Shay."

"Did he?" She kept her voice very low-key. Towe had been in the back of her mind all the time she had

47

been riding, but she didn't want to let on to her mother that she was upset with him.

"You don't sound very interested."

"Of course I'm interested. What did he want?"

"He didn't say. But he did say he'd call back later."

"Fine."

"Shay, do you know a Randy Russell?"

Shay felt her heart race for a moment. How had her mother happened to ask about Randy? "Yes, Mom. I met him last night. I told you. He's Mollie's cousin, the one who wants to be a vet. He's in town for some sort of meeting at the university."

"He wrote you a note." Her mother nodded toward a white envelope propped against the sugar bowl on the drop-leaf table.

"You're kidding!" Shay hurried to the table and picked up the envelope. It had only her name in the center and Randy's name in the upper left corner. It hadn't been mailed, so that meant he had delivered it personally. Randy Russell had stopped by her house to see her.

"Did you tell him where I was, Mom?"

"I didn't see him. Just found the envelope in the mailbox when I brought in the rest of the mail."

So he hadn't stopped to see her. He had just left the envelope. Her heart stopped pounding. But even so, he had been thinking of her, hadn't he? She ripped open the envelope as she headed toward her room for privacy. What could Randy be writing to her about?

Once her door was closed, she pulled the single folded sheet from the envelope and smoothed it flat.

Dear Shay,

It was fun talking with you last night at the D&D. We kidded around so much I forgot to tell you that I'm really interested in your mare and in her foal. When the time comes, I'd really appreciate it if you'd drop me a note and let me know the pertinent facts. Weight. Height. General condition of both mare and foal. I'd also be interested in any unusual facts about the birth, if there are any.

This may sound like a strange request, but I've been keeping records on horses since high-school days. A vet needs to know all he can about the type of animal he plans to work with. If you're willing to help, I'd appreciate it. Just write to me in care of the Sigma Rho house in Stillwater.

> Best,
> Randy

Shay read the letter twice; then she tucked it into the drawer of her desk, not knowing whether to be pleased or put down. Somehow she was getting the message that Randy Russell was more interested in her horse than he was in her. But what did she care? She pulled off her boots and changed into sneakers. She was Towe's steady. She wasn't looking for a new boyfriend. She would write to Randy when the time arrived. No big deal.

"How about some lunch?" her mother called from the kitchen. "Then this afternoon I want you to help me thin the carrots and weed the okra."

"Okay. What's for lunch?"

"Soup and salad. Soup's on the stove. Salad's in the refrig. Help yourself."

Shay helped herself to tomato soup and a cheese-and-pimento sandwich instead of a salad. She had just poured herself a glass of milk when the phone rang.

"You get it, will you, Shay?" her mother called from the back door. "It's probably Towe, and I'm already headed for the garden. Come on out when you're through talking."

Shay picked up the telephone, glad for privacy while she spoke. "Stuart residence, Shay speaking."

"Hi, Shay." Towe's voice sounded as if he might be right in the same room with her. The telephone was a sexy instrument, she thought. Sometimes she felt closer to Towe when they talked on the phone and his voice was right in her ear than she felt when they talked in person and he was only a few feet from her. But she was determined to keep her voice cool and aloof during this conversation. Hadn't Towe stood her up less than three hours ago?

4

The telephone line hummed for a few moments, and Shay cleared her throat. "Hi, Towe." She said no more, waited for him to speak.

"Hey, Shay, I don't blame you for being bent out of shape about this morning. I'm really sorry I couldn't keep our date, and I did call earlier. Didn't your mom tell you I tried to get you?"

"Mom said you called." She felt no guilt at letting him squirm a bit. She had squirmed plenty, hadn't she? Both last night and this morning. He had embarrassed her in front of her family, in front of Mollie.

"There was a bad smashup out on the highway south of the city early this morning, Shay. I had to go out with Dad in the wrecker and try to help. Nobody was seriously hurt, but both cars were totaled. It took a long time to get them separated and hauled back to town."

"I understand." She sighed. She did understand. Towe hadn't deliberately left her waiting.

"Shay, I would have called you if I could have. There weren't any telephones for miles, and Dad needed me on the spot."

"I said I understood."

"But you don't sound as if you understood. Give a guy a break, huh?"

Shay hesitated. She wanted to tell him that of course she understood, yet something made her hold back. Maybe if she hadn't seen him at the D&D with the guys yesterday afternoon she would feel differently.

"I'll make it up to you tonight," Towe said. "Why don't we go out to the Rose Room for dinner before we take in the flick?"

"Oh, Towe, you needn't take me anyplace so fancy. You'll never get your vo-tech tuition saved if you blow your money on dinners at the Rose Room." Now she let her voice grow warmer, but she knew she wasn't leveling with Towe. She really didn't want to go to the Rose Room. It wasn't a place where the high-school kids went. But his thought was sincere, she felt sure of that. "Why don't we just have a burger and fries at the D&D?"

"I feel really lousy about this morning, Shay. I want to do something special for you. A burger at the D&D is no big deal."

"I think it is. A burger with you is a big deal no matter where we have it. I missed you this morning, Towe, but I knew something had come up that you couldn't help."

"I was hoping you'd understand." Relief filled his voice. "See you around six this evening, okay?"

"Okay."

"See you."

"Right." She replaced the receiver, feeling like her old self again. Towe hadn't stood her up intentionally. She had known he wouldn't do a thing like that. Hadn't she? Why had a small part of her mind doubted?

"Shay?" her mother called from the garden. "Bring a paring knife when you come out, will you?"

"Sure, Mom. Be right there."

The afternoon passed quickly, in spite of the gardening. Once she got into the work she found it pleasant, and it allowed her time to daydream about Dancer and the horse show, about Towe and their date that night, about Randy Russell and the note.

That night, as she dressed for her date with Towe, she had a desire—no, it was more of a need—to look very special. She felt almost the same way she had felt before her first date with him. She wanted to look her very best, wanted him to be proud to be seen with her. What should she wear? She stood in front of her open closet considering her rather meager wardrobe. It seemed to her that most of the kids had more clothes than she did.

Should she wear the green jumper and the gingham blouse that brought out the green in her eyes? Sometimes she got sick of bringing out her eyes, but she lifted the jumper from its hanger and held it under her chin for effect. No. Too dressy. Not that it was really dressy. It was just that most of the kids never wore anything but jeans and shirts—dress jeans, of course, for Saturday night.

She pulled out her newest jeans, teamed them with a pink-and-white shirt. And she had pink canvas shoes to match the shirt. Would a pink ribbon holding her hair back be just too, too much? She tried it and decided that it would. Brushing her hair until it gleamed, she let it hang loose, wishing the bangs would hurry up and grow out.

Usually she didn't use much makeup, but tonight she applied a creamy foundation and topped it with some blusher that matched the lip gloss Mollie had given her for Christmas. As she stood in front of the mirror studying the effect, she hoped it was subtle enough to make Towe think she looked smashing, without making him think she had taken great pains to achieve the effect.

"Towe's here," her mother called to her a few moments later.

Shay jumped up. She hadn't heard him knock. She slung her denim bag over her shoulder and hurried to the living room. Towe was sitting on the green velvet couch with his long legs stretched under the coffee table, and when he saw her he nearly upset the table trying to get to his feet. Sometimes Towe reminded her of a colt still growing, awkward, yet charming. Tonight his brown, fawnlike eyes looked at her thoughtfully with an expression she couldn't understand. Was he still worried about this morning?

"Hi," she said with a broad smile. "Ready to go?"

"If you are." He took in her outfit with a glance. "You look really neat tonight."

"Thanks. So do you." Shay noted Towe's new-faded jeans, his light blue shirt. Some girls complained because their boyfriends never gave them a compliment, but she couldn't say that about Towe. He usually noticed what she wore, and he usually commented. It always gave her a lift, yet she knew she shouldn't need compliments to give her assurance. She should have more faith in herself. But somehow she didn't. If it weren't for Towe and Mollie, she would be a complete zero. Nobody would notice her. Even Randy Russell had only noticed her horse.

They left the house, and Towe opened the car door for her.

"I see you got the parts all back in it," Shay said.

"Right. It works a lot better than it did. And I learned a lot. Sometimes I think I could learn more by working for Dad at his shop than I could learn at vo-tech school. It'd save a bundle of money, too."

"Then why don't you just do that?" Shay hated to think of Towe graduating in a few weeks and leaving her in the fall. What would she do during a whole year of high school without him? Would he come home every weekend?

"Dad thinks I need to go away to school. He's not much on diesel engines, and he thinks they may be the thing of the future. I suppose he's right." Towe pulled a wrench from his shirt pocket and laid it on the dashboard. "Guess I won't need that tonight."

"I hope not." Shay laughed. Then she sobered as Towe drove past the D&D and on to the Rose Room at the very edge of the city. "Hey, I thought we decided—"

"*You* decided." Towe grinned and took her hand in his. "Give a guy a break, Shay. If I hadn't wanted to take you to the Rose Room, I wouldn't have asked you, okay?"

"Okay." She laughed and squeezed his hand. "But I'm going to order lobster stuffed with crabmeat, and we may both have to wash dishes to pay the bill."

"I think you mean crab stuffed with lobster, don't you?"

They laughed together all the time Towe was parking the car, and when they entered the Rose Room they were still smiling. From the outside the building looked like any other concrete-block building, but on the inside the restaurant lived up to its name. The walls were painted a hot pink, the thick carpeting was a deep red, and a pink linen cloth and a crystal bowl with a single rose decorated every dining table. Rose fragrance scented the whole dining area. They waited until a hostess wearing an ankle-length pink gown led them to a table for two in a secluded alcove and placed menus before them.

"What would you like?" Towe asked.

"What are you going to have?" Shay peered nervously at the menu, keeping her head down so Towe wouldn't see her glancing at the right-hand column of prices.

"Our special tonight is the veal with mushrooms," the waitress suggested.

"That'll be fine for me," Towe said.

"I'll have that, too," Shay agreed, thinking she would much rather be having a cheeseburger and fries at the D&D.

"It's really great here, Towe." Shay inhaled deeply of the rose scent.

"Right. So enjoy."

They had to wait a long time before their meal arrived, and as other, older couples began filling the tables around them Shay began to feel conspicuous in her blue jeans and gingham shirt. She had honestly thought they were heading for the D&D, otherwise she would have worn her jumper. She was glad they were seated; the tablecloth hid most of their clothes. When the waitress brought their salads, they helped themselves to the dressing, then ate slowly, setting the bowls aside when they finished.

"Looks as if we're going to miss the first show." Towe glanced at his watch. "I didn't know they were so slow in here."

"What time is it?"

"Already almost seven. But we can make the second flick. If the second show starts at nine, we should be out by eleven or eleven-thirty. We'll still have thirty minutes to meet your curfew."

"Yeah, I guess that's right." She had hated to discuss her curfew until she learned that Towe had one, too. Now that subject didn't bother either of them.

They talked little during the meal. The veal was tender and good, and the baked potato with sour cream was delicious. Shay felt as if she couldn't eat another bite by the time her plate was bare, but Towe ordered dessert.

They reached the movie just as the early show was letting out. Shay saw Beth and Sue together; then Mollie and Chip came out, laughing and holding hands. Chip was short and stocky, about the same height as Mollie, and he always had a package of saxophone reeds sticking from his shirt pocket. Chip played with the Rockin' Five, and he didn't want anyone to forget it. When Mollie saw Shay, she came over to the velvet rope that separated the incoming and outgoing lines.

"Hey, where were you? We looked all over the theater for you two."

"Yeah, where were you, man?" Chip asked Towe. "Thought we were going to hit Lunny's after the flick."

"Another time, Chip," Towe said. "We just finished having dinner."

"Dinner, yet." Mollie grinned. "Well, la-di-da."

"Why don't you just shag out to Lunny's with us and forget the flick?" Chip asked. "The whole gang's going to be there, and there's a special rock band playing tonight. They may let me sit in for a few numbers."

Towe held up their tickets. "Just bought the tickets. Maybe we'll see you out there later, okay?"

"Deal," Mollie said. "We'll be looking for you."

Shay said nothing. She would just as soon have gone on out to Lunny's; Towe could have gotten a refund on the tickets. Lunny's was a special Saturday-night place where the high-school crowd went, a step up from the D&D. But, on the other hand, Shay knew she would enjoy sitting beside Towe in the movie without anyone else around to claim their attention.

"Where shall we sit?" Towe asked as they headed down the aisle.

"Wherever you want to. It doesn't matter to me." She hoped he would choose seats to the back in sort of a secluded spot, but he didn't. He went front and center, and when the screen lighted up with the coming attractions, she felt as if someone had turned a spotlight on them. But it didn't matter. Not many people had come to the second show. The theater was almost empty. Towe reached for her hand when the regular feature started, and she settled back to enjoy the show, to enjoy having Towe near.

During the opening of the plot Towe had a coughing spell. He withdrew his hand from hers as he pulled a handkerchief from his pocket.

"Are you all right?" Shay asked, wondering if she should pound him on the back. Was he choking?

"I'm okay. Excuse me a minute? Got to get a drink."

It seemed to her that Towe was gone a long time, but when he returned he was no longer coughing. She smiled up at him, and he smiled back, but when he sat down again, he didn't take her hand.

After the movie ended and they had filed into the lobby, Shay excused herself to go to the rest room. It had been such a strange evening. First the dinner at the Rose Room, surrounded by adults, then the movie, with none of their friends near. She glanced at her watch. Just eleven o'clock. She still had an hour before curfew.

A glance into the mirror told her she needed to refresh her makeup, comb her hair. She pushed down on her bangs, then combed them to one side. She wished she had brought her purse-size cologne. Towe liked the lilac fragrance, and although she had touched dabs onto her throat before she left home, the scent had evaporated long ago.

Shay smiled as she stepped from the rest room, expecting to see Towe waiting for her, but instead she saw Towe and Ginger Netherton standing near the popcorn machine. Ginger had on copper-colored satin jeans and a satin shirt that fitted her the way a grape skin fits a grape. She was standing with one hand on Towe's arm, and when she saw Shay, she smiled up at Towe, winked, and sauntered out the theater door.

"What was that all about?" Shay kept her voice light, but she felt a coldness inside her. Instinctively she knew that Ginger and Towe had been talking about last night, about last night and the handsome stranger in the booth with her and Mollie at the D&D.

"Nothing important." Towe followed Ginger with his eyes. "She just stopped to say hi."

"Sure."

"Jealous?"

"No way," she lied. She kept smiling, still trying for a light mood, but now Towe didn't smile back. She stuck her hands into the pockets of her cord blazer, waiting for Towe to make the next move, the next comment.

"Want to join the gang at Lunny's?"

"Sure." She glanced at her watch again. "We've got almost an hour. But do you suppose anyone's still there?"

"Yeah. The gang won't leave until Lunny closes the place."

Towe held the car door for her, and she slid onto the front seat. Lunny's was near Oral Roberts U., and it took them only a few minutes to reach it. Towe turned into the parking lot and drove slowly, as if looking for a slot, yet he passed three without stopping. Shay decided he must be looking for cars that he recognized.

"There's Chip's old Chevy." She pointed. "Guess he and Mollie are still inside." Towe said nothing, and she pointed to another car. "There's Jason King's VW. I think he and Sue were doubling with Beth and Arnie tonight." Suddenly she realized their conversation was totally one-sided. She stopped talking. Towe circled the parking lot another time before he spoke.

"Do you really want to go in?"

"Only if you do, Towe. It doesn't really matter to me all that much."

"I thought it might not matter at all."

She looked at Towe, wondering how she should respond to his comment. "I don't know what you mean, Towe. If you don't want to go in, we can go on home. I baked some cookies this afternoon. Your favorites— chocolate chip. We can have cookies and milk."

"Let's go. I want to talk with you anyway."

"Fine. It's really pretty late to be going into Lunny's. By the time we got our order we'd have to hurry eating it if I were to get home on time." Shay sensed that she was chattering aimlessly, which wasn't her usual habit. What did Towe want to talk with her about? Something that Ginger had told him? She could guess what that was. But maybe not. Sometimes Ginger bluffed—bluffed until the other person tipped his hand and ended up feeling needlessly foolish. She wasn't going to let Ginger do that to her. If anyone mentioned Ginger, it would have to be Towe.

But why look at the dark side? Maybe Towe wanted to talk about his class ring. Maybe he was going to ask her to wear it. And maybe he wanted to do the asking in the privacy of her own home. But somehow she doubted that.

As long as they were going to talk, she could think of a few pertinent subjects, too. The wax job on the car, for one. She scowled. Why was she borrowing problems? It was late. They would have had to hurry if they had stopped at Lunny's. That was why Towe had passed it by.

The night was chilly, colder than the day had been, but the moon was full now and it silvered the pecan trees in the yard, silvered the red tile of the roof, leaving part of it in shadow where the pecan branches hung low. When Towe turned into the driveway and cut the motor, the night was silent except for the distant baying of a hound, the cry of an owl which seemed to be right in the pecan tree.

Shay waited for Towe to get out, to come around and open her door; then, when he didn't do that, she waited for him to take her hand. But he didn't do that, either. What was wrong? What had he and Ginger been talking about? Her stomach felt as if she had drunk ten glasses of ice water and it was sloshing inside her in a deep, frigid pool.

"Shall we go in, Towe?"

"Okay." He got out, came around to her side of the car, opened the door.

"I suppose the folks are asleep, but I'm sure we won't bother them." Why was she chattering again? They went inside lots of times after her parents had retired. It was no big deal.

"Maybe we'd better just sit on the porch." Towe sat down on a plastic-covered glider and waited for her to join him.

"I'll go get the cookies, okay?"

"I'm really not hungry, Shay. That dinner was really filling."

"Towe, that dinner was hours ago. I'm hungry and I'm going to have some cookies, okay?"

"Okay."

She went inside, picked up the cookie tin, and carried it to the porch. Towe took a cookie when she offered it, and she took one. How stilted and strange everything seemed. If he wanted to talk about something Ginger had said, he was certainly slow in bringing it up. And she wasn't going to help him. If he didn't trust her, why, that was his problem. But did she trust him? And if she trusted him, why did seeing him at the D&D when he said he was going to be waxing a car bother her?

Suddenly her mouth was so dry she could hardly swallow the cookie. "I'm going to get us some milk, Towe." She stood. "Or would you rather have a cola?"

"Either one's okay."

She brought out colas and ice-filled glasses, poured the drinks, and waited. Now there was no sound except ice tinkling against glass. When the silence between them became unbearable, she spoke up.

"The first horse show of the season is coming up two weeks from today, Towe."

"You've mentioned that."

"I thought maybe you'd forgotten. Are you planning to come watch me ride?"

"I might."

"I'm sorry that it falls on a day when we usually do something together, but if you come to the show, then we can do something afterward, okay?"

"We'll see."

"Towe, what's the matter? If something's wrong, let's bring it out in the open and talk about it, okay?" She hesitated several seconds, then blurted, "What did Ginger tell you?"

"That she saw you with another boy at the D&D last night. Are you going to say she was lying?"

Good old Ginger, Shay thought, scowling. "She wasn't lying, Towe. She was at the D&D last night. She saw me with another boy."

"Who?"

"Before I tell you that, I want you to know that she also saw Mollie there with that same boy. Did she mention that?"

"No. She didn't say anything about Mollie."

"I didn't think so." She almost told Towe that she was disappointed in him because he didn't trust her; then she remembered her own feelings about him, her own doubts about seeing him at the D&D with the guys yesterday afternoon. "Do you want to hear the whole story, or do you prefer to hear just Ginger's version?"

For a moment Towe hesitated. Too long a moment?

Did he really prefer to know just Ginger's view of what had happened?

"I guess Ginger just surprised me, Shay. But you're not on the witness stand, for Pete's sake. You've a perfect right to go to the D&D with anyone you choose."

Again Shay waited, considering Towe's response carefully. He acted almost disappointed to hear about Mollie. She couldn't zero in on a clear translation of his response. *Translation?* Yes, that was a good word for what she was seeking, a translation. She and Towe didn't seem to be speaking the same language tonight. Now she considered her own words thoughtfully and carefully.

"Towe, we're acting crazy. And all because of Ginger. Can't you *see* what she's trying to do? She's trying to cause trouble between us. I was at the D&D with Mollie, and the boy with us was Randy Russell. He's Mollie's cousin, who's in town for a meeting at Tulsa U."

"Oh."

Shay let Towe's *oh* roll around on her eardrums for a few seconds. Disappointment? Certainly not anger. Relief? Again she felt she couldn't translate his tone into anything meaningful to her.

" 'Oh'? Is that all you have to say, Towe? Just 'Oh'?"

"What did you expect me to say?"

"I didn't expect to even be discussing the subject."

"Then you weren't going to mention anything about this Randy Russell?"

"I don't know. I might have. If we had met Mollie and Chip at Lunny's, Randy's name might have come up in the conversation. I would probably have asked how he liked T.U. That would have been a natural question, I think. Towe, it's not like you to be jealous."

"I'm not jealous, not really. I guess I just let Ginger flap me."

Shay shivered. Why were they sitting outside when it was so cool? Why hadn't she brought out hot chocolate instead of colas? Was she going to do everything wrong? "I guess Ginger got the reaction she wanted." Shay wished she hadn't said that. Mollie had tried to help her figure Ginger out, and Mollie's advice had been for Shay never to act the least bit insecure about Towe's steadfast affection. *Steadfast affection*. Those were Mollie's exact words. Sometimes Mollie really sounded like a psychology book.

Towe made no response to her comment about Ginger. Shay finished her cola and offered Towe another cookie. When he refused the cookie, she stood.

"I guess I'd better be going in now, Towe. It was a grand evening until . . ."

". . . until Ginger showed up, huh?" Towe stood, too. "I'm sorry, Shay. I should have paid no attention to her. Sometimes she does try to start trouble. It was really a neat evening."

"I'm glad you understand about Randy, Towe. You're the only boy for me. How could you ever doubt that?"

"My fault. It won't happen again, okay?"

"Okay."

When Towe took her in his arms, she went willingly, pressing her head against his chest. She could hear his heart thudding, and she wondered if he could hear hers. He held her for a few seconds, and she could feel his warm breath in her hair, and on her forehead; then she lifted her face to him for his kiss, and as his lips touched hers gently, tenderly, she knew that all was well between them. It would take more than a girl like Ginger Netherton to break them up.

When they parted, Towe opened the screen door for her, and she stood just inside the entryway, looking out at him. He had just stepped off the porch, and the moonlight played fiery lights onto his red hair.

"Towe, you *will* come to watch me ride in the show, won't you?"

"Two weeks from today, you say?"

"Right." She held herself very still, not exactly holding her breath, but breathing very softly. She had expected an instant acceptance. They had a standing date for Saturday nights. Why was he hesitating?

"Don't know if I can make it to the show or not, Shay. You see, I have this uncle who's coming to visit us that weekend—just for that day, in fact. I've got to be home to see him."

"Can't you see him in the morning? See him over the dinner table? Do you have to see him all afternoon, too? I want you at the arena cheering for me, Towe."

"I wish I could say yes. I really do. But Uncle Bill's a car nut, too. He's offered to show me how to do a professional valve job on my car."

"Your dad could show you that, couldn't he?"

"He could, but he's so busy at the shop that he never seems to have time. But Uncle Bill, now, that's a different thing. I really can't pass up the opportunity."

"I see," Shay said, not seeing at all.

"Hey, I'm really sorry, Shay. And if we get through with the valve job in time, we'll both come out to the show ring, okay? Uncle Bill likes horses, too."

"But cars come first," Shay said.

"Well, sure, cars come first. It's just like horses come first with you. Hey, no hard feelings, okay?"

"Okay. No hard feelings." She watched as Towe turned and hurried to his car. Then he glanced back and waved. "See ya, Shay."

5

See ya, Shay. The three words echoed in Shay's mind as she locked the door, snapped off the living-room lights, went to her room. *See ya, Shay.* She blinked rapidly to keep tears from coming and spilling down her cheeks. What was the problem between her and Towe? Sure, Ginger had blabbed to him about Randy; but, in all fairness, she had to admit that she had felt a tension between them even before that. *See ya, Shay.* For weeks Towe had not left her without setting a time and place for their next meeting, even when it fell on one of their usual date nights. But tonight he had set up no definite time for their next date.

Maybe he had been distracted, she thought. It had been such an unusual evening. They seldom went out to dinner, and they usually went to the movies with a whole gang of kids. Maybe Towe would call her in the morning.

It took her a long time to fall asleep that night, and in the morning she was the first one up and about. She pretended great interest in the Sunday paper, but all the time her eyes were reading the headlines, her ears were listening for the phone to ring.

"How about waffles this morning, Shay?" her mother asked. "I'll mix the batter if you'll bake them."

"Deal." Shay laid the paper aside and began setting the table for breakfast.

"Have a good time last night?" Her dad yawned and sat down at the drop-leaf table, although breakfast was still quite a few minutes in the future.

"Yes," Shay replied. "We had a good time." How did one define a good time? To her parents, a dinner at the Rose Room followed by a movie would be a good time. But was it a good time if your date clammed up like a . . . like a *clam?* Was it a good time if he avoided going places where your regular friends were having fun? Was it a good time if he just said "See ya" when he left?

"You don't sound too excited about it," her mother said.

"Just still sleepy, I guess," Shay said. Her parents were wearing tan corduroy robes, matching robes that made them look more than ever like twins. And the robes told her they were going to church later and were waiting until that time to get dressed.

She mixed frozen juice, which they drank while her mother finished measuring the ingredients for the waffle batter; then Shay plugged in the waffle iron and took over the waffle baking, all the time hoping for the phone to ring, hoping Towe would call her.

They ate waffles until the batter was gone. Waffles with jam. Waffles with maple syrup. Waffles with honey. And still the phone didn't ring.

"I'll clean up the kitchen," her father said after they had finished eating. "My turn."

"I won't argue." Her mother went to the living room and picked up the women's section of the paper.

"Me, either." Shay tried to sound pleasant, but it wasn't easy. The telephone continued its silence, and she was glad when it was time to dress for church.

She half hoped Towe would call while she was out. But that was crazy. She wanted to talk to him, didn't she? Maybe he would be at church. Maybe he would come sit with her. She liked it when he wore his western dress suit and string tie, his hand-tooled dress boots.

Shay dressed more carefully than usual, wearing her avocado-green blouse with her green-and-gold plaid skirt. She brushed her long hair until it gleamed, then tied it back with a velvet ribbon that matched her blouse. Green and gold. She glanced in the mirror, feeling very well put together. She usually felt that way on her own turf. But when she left home and saw other kids and began comparing herself unfavorably with the other girls, she always felt as if she were about to come apart.

Why did she make such comparisons? It was a crazy thing to do. She had talked with Mollie about it, and Mollie had said she should only compare herself to *herself* and try to be the best self she could be. Good advice. But she had trouble carrying it out. She was glad when they were in the car, on their way to church. She kept seeing Towe in her mind, kept reliving the strange tension that had grown between them in the past two days.

Hymns. Anthem. Scripture readings. Baptisms. Shay felt as if they had had the full course before the minister even stepped to the pulpit to begin the sermon. Even then she couldn't concentrate on his words. She inhaled the scent of burning candles, watched sunshine streaming through the stained-glass windows.

When the church service ended, she walked to the car and waited for her parents. They always stood around talking with friends, but she was in no mood to do that today. Maybe if Towe had been there it would have been different. But he hadn't been there. *See ya, Shay.* When did he mean he would see her?

"How about grilling hamburgers and eating on the patio?" her father asked when they had returned from church and changed into casual clothes.

"Suits me," her mother said. "I've creamed potatoes. Shay, would you make a coleslaw?"

"Okay." Shay reached for the cabbage grater. "You want it sweet or tart?"

"Somewhere in between, okay?" Her mother carried a red-and-white-checked cloth to the redwood picnic table in the backyard, then returned to the kitchen for the red plastic dishes.

How could a telephone be so silent? Shay glared at the instrument as it hung on the kitchen wall. Silence. Well, she wouldn't sit around waiting for Towe to call today. No way. She flounced outside.

"Shay, you're not eating your share," her dad said as they sat around the picnic table and he looked at her plate. "Feeling okay?"

"I'm fine. Guess that big dinner last night really filled me up." She made an effort to finish her hamburger. Sometimes her father got uptight about his outdoor cooking unless everyone ate as though they were breaking a two-week fast.

"The coleslaw's delicious, Shay," her mother said.

"Thanks, Mom. I aim to please. Eat your heart out, Julia Child." She tried to keep up some banter, pretend that everything in her life was peachy keen. But she knew that if her parents said one word about Towe Williams she might burst into tears of anger and frustration. Boys! Who could understand them?

They had just finished clearing the table and straightening the kitchen when Shay heard a car pull into the driveway, heard a horn honk. It was a tinny sound, like the honk of a car on the Saturday-morning TV cartoons. She knew without looking that it wasn't Towe.

"Were you going out with the girls this afternoon, Shay?" her mother asked. "Looks like Sue and Beth and Mollie out front in that VW convertible of Sue's."

"I had planned to go riding—riding on Dancer, Mom." She hurried out the door to see what the girls wanted, stopping for a moment in surprise as she saw all three of them still dressed in their go-to-church clothes.

"What's up?" she called as she strolled toward the car. Mollie was wearing a bright orange jumper with a balloon-sleeved white blouse, and with her black hair she projected a Halloween effect. Sue had on a rust-colored sheath dress that slimmed her pudgy figure and blended with her sandy hair and freckles, and Beth was wearing a full-skirted peasant-style dress that went well with her Dutch bob, round cheeks, and blue eyes.

"We need one more guide," Mollie said.

"Guide for what?" Shay asked.

"There's a special open house at Philbrook Art Center this afternoon," Mollie said. "It's sponsored by the Civic Club, but some of their guides have bagged out on them. They called my mom to see if she could scare up some replacements."

"And you three are who she scared up!" Shay smiled at them. "You look very grand."

"Doesn't hurt a girl to dress up now and then," Sue said. "Come on with us, Shay. Throw on your Sunday threads and hop in."

"Can't do it," Shay said. "Got plans."

"Towe figures in the plans, no doubt," Beth said, sighing.

Shay saw Mollie looking at her, waiting for her answer. "What's going on at Philbrook?" she asked, trying to divert the subject from Towe.

"Just a tour of the gallery and formal gardens," Mollie said. "Open house and all that. Lots of people right here in Tulsa have never seen inside the place, either when the Phillips family lived there or since it's been turned into an art gallery. Come on with us, Shay. A little culture never hurt anyone."

"There'll be punch and cake." Sue grinned until her freckles danced.

"And maybe boys," Beth said. "Mom says some college prof is requiring his art class to take the tour and write a paper on the Indian baskets and pottery on exhibit there. I wouldn't mind guiding some neat college guy through the place."

"I really can't do it this afternoon." Shay shook her head, hating to turn the girls down. A few months ago she would have popped a seam to accept such an invitation, she would have been so glad and so flattered to have anyone interested in her. But things were different now.

"That Towe!" Sue grumbled. "Maybe we could get him to serve as a guide, too. Then you'd come along, I'll bet."

"I'm not going out with Towe," Shay said at last. "I've got a date with a horse. There's a show coming up in a couple of weeks, and Dancer and I have to practice for it."

"Yuck, Shay!" Beth wrinkled her nose. "It's always either Towe or a horse. You don't give your girlfriends the time of day anymore."

"You're welcome to come out to the stable," Shay said. "You can even ride Dancer if you want to. I'll work her for only a short time, and then you can pleasure ride. Why don't you drop out after the tour ends?"

"Let's do," Mollie said to the others. "How about it?"

"Maybe," Beth said. Then she turned to Shay again. "We'll see, okay? Maybe we'll join you later."

"Deal." Shay grinned as they waved and Sue backed the VW from the driveway. Why hadn't she gone with them? She could spare the time. She would have plenty of time to work Dancer later in the evening. She sighed, knowing why she had refused. She wanted to be where Towe could find her easily. He would never think of looking for her at Philbrook, and even if her folks told him she was there, he probably wouldn't bother to dress up and come there to meet her.

"Going to the stable?" her dad asked when she returned to the house.

"Yes." Shay glanced at her watch. "Got to get busy out there if I expect to win any trophies this summer."

"Want us to drive you out?" her mother asked. "We might watch you ride for a while."

Shay thought for a moment. If her parents drove her to the stable, then she would have no transportation home. Of course, they probably thought Towe would come out to bring her home, but she knew she couldn't depend on that. Not today. Maybe not any day.

"I think I'll just ride my bike, Mom. I need the exercise."

"Should think riding the horse would be enough exercise," her mother said.

"Well, bike riding's a different kind of exercise. You know." Shay hurried to the garage for her bike before anyone could argue, waved goodbye, and pedaled down the street.

The sun warmed her as she rode along the city streets, then turned onto the blacktop that led to Redhill Ranch. The smell of new-mown hay hung across the countryside. She saw great rolls of the green stuff dotting a field on her left. In another pasture three Hereford cows stood belly deep in the bottle-green water of a pond. So much for Blackberry Winter, she thought with a laugh. Cows cooling themselves in ponds were a sure sign of summer. On her left a blue jay screamed and darted into a linden tree, and a crow cawed as it circled a weathered red barn on her right.

When she reached the stable, she was surprised to see Dancer tethered to a hitching rail, and it was a moment before she noticed Dr. Richards standing on the mare's far side. She approached the pair, reaching to pat Dancer on the head.

"Hello, girl," she crooned. "And hello, Dr. Richards." She smiled at the vet, who was packing a bag of equipment and preparing to leave. The middle-aged doctor was short, and he looked stout even in his vertically striped coverall. He had a fringe of gray hair that reminded Shay of a Brillo pad, but the center of his head was bald. The sun gleamed against his bald spot, giving it the appearance of having been waxed. But what had made her think of that? She wanted to forget anything that pertained to wax or waxing. She concentrated on Dr. Richard's eyes, which were warm and blue and friendly.

"Glad you stopped by today, Shay," Dr. Richards said. "I was going to call you. Sorry I had to be away yesterday."

"How is Dancer?" Shay asked. "Everything okay?"

"Everything's fine, so far."

Shay caught an ominous tone in the vet's voice and was instantly alert. "Is something the matter? What about the foal? When do you expect it to arrive?"

Dr. Richards picked up his bag of instruments, patted Dancer on the withers, then faced Shay. "This may turn out to be a very unusual case, Shay. I've not had much experience with multiple births in horses, but—"

"Multiple births?" Shay almost shouted the words. "You mean Dancer may have more than one foal?"

"I think that may be the case." The doctor nodded. "I want to have Doc Jenkins take a look at her the next time he's out this way. Always good to have a second opinion."

"Twins!" Shay shouted and threw her arm around Dancer's neck. "Twins! How exciting."

"Hold on a minute before you go into a joy jig."

Again an ominous tone in Dr. Richards' voice silenced Shay. "What are you trying to tell me? Is Dancer in danger? The foals?"

"Now don't go a-worrying about Dancer," Dr. Richards said. "But you should know that the incidence of multiple births in horses is mighty rare. Mighty rare. And sometimes there are complications."

"What sort of complications?" Shay asked, her voice so quiet she could hear her heart beating.

"Sometimes it requires special care of the mare to bring both foals through the birth in good shape."

"What can we do? I'll do whatever you say, Doctor. Does she need special food, special medicine?"

"I'll take care of all that, Shay. I know you plan to enter shows this summer, and I hate to tell you this, but in my opinion, Dancer should not be ridden anymore until after she gives birth."

"Oh." Shay could hardly believe she had heard right. She owned a registered horse. She had spent hours learning how to ride it with western tack. And now she couldn't ride.

"Maybe you could rent a horse from the stable," Dr. Richards suggested. "That's always a possibility."

"Yes. Sure. I'll ask about it."

"Of course you can groom Dancer just as you always do. You can come see her, lead her around the pasture at a walk. But she has no business working in the show ring for the next few weeks."

"All right, Doctor. I don't want to do anything that isn't good for her."

"I knew you'd understand, Shay. And when the foals arrive, it'll be worth all your sacrifice. You'll see."

The doctor got into his panel truck and left the stable, and Shay just stood there for a few minutes patting Dancer, trying to adjust to the news she had just heard.

"Tough luck, Shay."

Shay whirled about to face Eric Chapin; then she stood there speechless, not knowing quite what to say. She felt close to tears, but she didn't want this stranger to see her crying. How she wished Towe were here. Where was he when she needed him?

"Well, it's not so tough, I suppose." Shay forced a smile of sorts. "Maybe I'll be able to rent a horse to ride in the shows. And just think—two foals. That's really exciting. The doctor said it was very unusual."

"Yeah," Eric agreed. "So unusual that one foal usually doesn't survive. A mare carrying twins is just a big bother to everyone."

"But sometimes the foals both survive, don't they?" Shay asked. "Sometimes?"

"Yeah, Sometimes, I suppose." Eric hunched along on his crutches, trying to balance himself on his good foot while he curried one side of Cherokee.

Shay led Dancer to the pasture gate and turned her out to graze. When she walked back to the stable, Eric was still there. She wished he hadn't told her about twin foals being so high risk. Yet in a way she was glad to know; she would be even more careful with Dancer.

"Can I help you with that?" Shay asked as she watched Eric struggling to groom his horse.

"I can do everything except his feet," he said. "Would you mind? I hate to think of him walking on stones and stuff."

"Sure." Then Shay backed off a bit. "He doesn't kick, does he?"

"Hardly ever."

She looked at Eric as she heard the note of amusement in his voice. Today the sun shone on his dark hair, making it look like polished bronze, and his green eyes held a twinkle she hadn't noticed before. She smiled at him.

"You're kidding, aren't you?"

"Yeah. Cherokee's gentle. I wouldn't let you touch him if he weren't. Say . . ."

Shay looked up at him again as he hesitated. "What?"

"Would you want to ride him? I mean, if you haven't got time, I'll understand, but I like to have him ridden a little every day, and with this dumb ankle I can't do it myself."

"Sure. I'll give him a turn around the pasture." Shay waited while Eric untied the reins from the hitching rail.

"How about giving him a few turns around the ring instead? I had planned to enter the shows this summer, too, and I may still be able to, later on when I can walk again. I don't want Cherokee to get out of practice."

"Okay. I'll give him a few turns around the ring. You want to call the signals?"

"Deal."

Shay mounted the gelding while Eric swung on his crutches, lurching toward the arena gate. She rode Cherokee around the ring several times, changing gaits as Eric called out the signals. She liked this horse. His trot was almost as smooth as Dancer's, and he took his leads correctly and without breaking stride. For the first time she realized how tough it was going to be to win a trophy. She realized that just because Dancer went so well in the ring she had been underestimating her competition.

"Hey, thanks a lot," Eric said when Shay left the arena and tethered Cherokee to the hitching rail once more.

"He's really a nice mount, Eric. Smooth. And well behaved."

"I trained him myself," Eric said proudly. "Been working with him for four years now."

"Where did you live before you moved to Tulsa?" she asked.

"Lawton. Home of Fort Sill, Geronimo, and Eric Chapin."

"Who helped you train Cherokee?" Shay was surprised at how easy it was to talk to Eric. It was as if she had known him for years instead of just for days.

"An old retired cavalryman lived near us in Lawton. He taught me a lot of horse sense."

"He must have. I think horses are really pretty dumb, but you've really done a great job training this one."

"Who says horses are dumb?" Eric stopped smiling and looked directly at Shay.

"Well, I don't think they are supersmart. Do you? I mean, they don't know when to stop eating, and they shy at the least little thing—like a crutch, for instance."

"Hold on just a darn minute." Eric smiled again. "I think a horse is the smartest creature on earth—at being a horse. It's only when you expect him to think like a human that a horse seems dumb."

Shay thought about that for a while, but before she could say anything one way or the other Eric continued.

"Their horse sense has helped them survive for ages. Lots of bigger, stronger animals disappeared, you know. Dinosaurs, for example."

Shay laughed. "Okay, so I shouldn't expect a horse to think like a human. Maybe they aren't so dumb, after all. Anyway, you've done a good job of training Cherokee." Shay glanced at her watch, feeling sure the girls weren't going to join her. "Thanks for letting me ride, Eric. I've got to get back home now."

"Can I give you a lift?" He nodded at the sky. "Some mighty dark clouds coming up in the west."

Shay glanced at the sky and heard distant thunder. Where had the sunshine gone? "I rode my bike."

Eric nodded at a white pickup truck. "If you can heave the bike into the truck bed, it won't be any problem."

"You mean you can drive okay with that foot?"

"Sure. Lucky it was my left ankle, though, or I'd really be out of it. How about it? I'd be glad to give you a ride home. Might save you from getting soaked."

"Okay. I'll take you up on it."

Eric lowered the truck's tailgate, and Shay managed to lift one wheel at a time until she got the bike into the bed. Then she got in on the passenger side of the cab, and Eric drove her home.

When they pulled into the driveway, her father hurried to the truck and helped unload the bicycle. "Care to come in, young man?"

"Dad, this is Eric Chapin; Eric, my father, Mr. Stuart."

"We've met," Eric said, smiling at her. "He's the one who gave me some dos and don'ts about this ankle, remember?"

Shay's father smiled. "And I have a feeling we'll meet again when you're walking without crutches once more."

"Thanks for the ride, Eric," Shay said, shutting off any more opportunities for her father to invite Eric inside.

"You're welcome, Shay. See ya."

See ya. Did all boys say that? She watched as the white truck drove from the driveway, and she realized she hadn't thought of Towe all afternoon. For a moment she felt guilty; then she put those thoughts from her mind. She guessed that she had probably thought about Towe just as much as he had thought about her. She hurried on inside just as the first sprinkles of rain began to fall.

"Towe called you while you were out," her mother said. "He asked if you'd call him when you came in."

Shay grinned in spite of herself. Towe had called! And he wanted her to call him back. Well, all right! That was more like it. She headed for the phone, then hesitated. Maybe she should make him wait awhile longer for her call. Maybe she shouldn't be so eager. But no. There was no pretending between her and Towe. She wasn't the coy type. What Towe saw was pretty much what he got. She picked up the receiver and dialed.

6

Towe answered the telephone on the second ring, and Shay wondered if he had been sitting at home waiting for her to call. Did boys do that sort of thing? Somehow she thought it was only girls who sat around with one ear tuned for a summons from Ma Bell.

"Hi, Towe," she replied. "My answering service recorded a message from you and a request for a reply, right?"

"Right." Towe cleared his throat. "You weren't in when I called."

"Obviously. But I'm in now."

"Obviously." He laughed, and a little of the tension between them was broken.

"Thought I might see you at church this morning or at the stable this afternoon." Shay paused, waiting for his response.

"Couldn't make it. Dad had some extra chores lined up for me. Did you have a good practice session in the ring?"

"Towe! Wait till I tell you!"

"I'm waiting. I'm waiting."

"Dr. Richards says Dancer may have twins. Twins! How about that?"

"Didn't know horses did things like that! I've never seen twin foals."

"Dr. Richards says it's really rare. Twins! That's the good news."

"Then I take it there's bad news, too?"

"I can't ride Dancer anymore until after she drops the foals. Dr. Richards said it would be better not to."

"Gee, Shay, I'm sorry about that. I mean, I know how much you had been counting on riding, winning."

"I may be able to work something out. You know, like maybe use a horse from the ranch."

"King?"

"Ugh! Don't know if I could manage that stallion or not. King's a lot of horse. You manage him nicely, but . . ."

"Maybe I could help you. Sometimes it's just a matter of showing him who's boss."

"Would you? Help me, I mean? Of course I'd have to ask Mr. Harmon. And I'm afraid he'll say no."

"Why?"

"Because he won't let Mollie rent King by the hour. He's afraid she'll get hurt. And Mollie's been riding western a lot longer than I have."

"But you ride better than Mollie does."

"You really think so?" Why was she so eager for his praise? His flattery? No, not flattery. Towe was usually sincere with her.

"Sure I think so, but you'll just have to ask Mr. Harmon and see what he says. But I didn't call you to talk about horses and shows."

"Oh?" She let the question hang between them, hoping she sounded interested, but not too interested.

"The gang's going to the D&D tomorrow after school for Cokes."

"So what else is new?" What was Towe leading up to? The gang usually went to the D&D after school—at least, a lot of them did.

"I want you to go with me, but I have to stay after class and talk to Miss Merton about last week's English assignment."

"I'll wait for you, okay? I have to return books to the library. I can do that while you're talking to Miss Merton."

"Deal. See ya then, okay?"

"Okay. See ya." She waited to hear him break the connection; then she hung up, too. A Coke date with Towe! And he had taken the time to call her about it. Usually they just met with sort of a mutual understanding. It gave the date more importance to have Towe call her ahead of time.

"Shay," her mother said when she had finished talking, "I couldn't help overhearing what you said about Dancer. How exciting!"

"Yeah, it really is. I just hate to miss out on riding her, but the foals will make it worthwhile. I'm not complaining."

At the Stuart house everyone was on his own for Sunday-night supper. Shay popped herself a huge bowl of popcorn, salted it, buttered it; then she grabbed an apple before she went to her room, leaving her parents still discussing Dancer. She sighed as she dropped onto her bed, thinking that this had been an almost perfect day. At least, it was hard to sort the imperfections from the perfections. A phone call from Towe was the perfect ending for almost any day.

After she had finished eating, Shay brushed her hair one hundred strokes, then brushed her bangs two hundred strokes extra to encourage their growth. Maybe she wouldn't mind them so much when they finally grew out, but right now they drove her bonkers. They were too short to pin back, but too long to hang free without getting in her eyes. But Towe was worth the annoyance.

The next day passed quickly. The state reading test took up most of the morning. She didn't see Towe, because only juniors were taking the test. Then afternoon classes were cut in half in order to allow makeup of the missed morning classes. Whenever there was a break in the regular school routine, time seemed to melt away. At the end of the school day Shay had hardly finished her errand in the library when Towe stopped for her, ready to go to the D&D.

"Get squared away with Miss Merton?" Shay asked.

"Yeah. Promised her I'd write an extra two pages if she wouldn't dock me for getting the paper in late."

"Sounds fair enough."

"I'll think so until I start slaving over the two pages." Towe laughed.

A light breeze cooled them as they walked toward the D&D, and Shay tried to enjoy it and the sunshine and not dwell on the fact that Towe had forgotten their dress code for the day. Of course, they didn't have clothes exactly alike, but they both wore jeans to school. And on Mondays they had agreed to wear their blue gingham shirts. On Tuesdays they wore red shirts, and although Towe's was a solid red and hers a red-and-white check, the effect was look-alike. On Wednesdays they wore white shirts, green on Thursdays, and plaid on Fridays. Today Towe was wearing a yellow T-shirt, and with her in blue gingham, their outfits looked totally unplanned.

"The place is already rocking," Shay said as Towe opened the door to the D&D and they stepped inside. She smelled the pipe smoke rising above two elderly men who sat at the horseshoe bar, waiting while Mr. Rogers hand-packed pints of ice cream for them. The booths at the sides of the bar were empty, but music, shouts, and laughter rose from the back of the building.

Towe slapped a dollar bill on the bar. "Could I get four quarters, please?"

Mr. Rogers opened the cash drawer, dropped the dollar inside, and scooped up four quarters, which he spilled into Towe's cupped hand.

"There you are, Towe. Take it easy back there. The old timbers will only stand so much." He winked, then turned his attention back to his older customers.

"Where shall we sit?" Shay asked, looking at the booths that surrounded the dance area.

"Hey, Shay! Towe! Over here," Mollie called to them.

"Guess that settles that decision." Towe laughed, took Shay's hand, and pulled her behind him as he threaded his way through dancers to the booth where Mollie and Chip were sitting.

"Where ya been?" Mollie shouted above the musical decibels which were hitting the walls like bullets and ricocheting back into the room.

"Had to stay after school," Towe shouted back. "No big deal. Did we miss anything?"

"Just more of the same," Chip said. "Skinny Ferris has played 'Rock Around the Clock' five times in a row.

Everyone's going to pound him if he plays it again, but I'm going to dance. Okay, Mollie?'' Chip stood, pushing two sax reeds farther down into his shirt pocket.

Mollie slid from the booth and joined Chip and the crowd on the dance floor. Shay watched for a while. It was hard to tell which kids were partners; each one seemed to be doing his own thing.

"Hey, look at Mollie," Shay said. "She's developed a neat step, and Chip's trying to imitate it."

"Look at those hips go." Towe whistled. "He'll work off a pound or two if he keeps that up."

The waitress took their order for colas; then Towe stood, offered his hand, and led Shay onto the floor. She and Towe sometimes practiced dance steps on Shay's front porch, and now they found a secluded corner and kept time to the rocking rhythm. Forward. Back. Shrug-shrug-point. Forward. Back . . .

Shay danced for a while with her eyes closed, and when she opened them she found that their corner was no longer secluded. She couldn't tell if she was dancing with Towe or with Beanie Goetz, it was that crowded. When the music stopped, Towe took her hand once more, and they returned to their booth.

"A real crowd today," Shay said.

"Yeah, but it's fun." Towe smiled at Mollie as she started to sit down. "Hey, Mollie. How about showing me that step you and Chip were doing?"

"Okay." Mollie shrugged. "Come on." Then she looked at Shay. "You don't mind, do you?"

"Of course she doesn't mind." Chip grabbed Shay's wrist. "But don't think we're going to sit here like crows on a fence while you two have all the fun. Come on, Shay. We'll show 'em."

Shay followed Chip onto the floor, and the number seemed to last forever. She felt strange dancing without Towe, and Chip's steps were ridiculous. Anyway, she felt ridiculous trying to follow them, imitate them. She just did her own thing, closing her eyes and pretending Towe was her partner.

When that number ended, some nerd paid a quarter for a blank record, three minutes of silence, but Shay didn't mind. She was ready to sit down and enjoy her cola. Now more kids had arrived, and they shared their booth with another couple, scrunching so close together that it was a relief when the music started again. Another girl claimed Towe for her partner, and the dancing became a gang scene, a mixer, with everyone switching partners.

"Grab someone," Mollie said as Shay returned to their booth. "Don't be a drag."

Shay smiled, but she didn't grab anyone. She sat down and sipped at the melted ice in the bottom of her glass, feeling very much out of it. When that disc ended, the kids on the floor changed partners and another tune started. This time Shay saw Towe dancing with Ginger Netherton, who was now wearing a yellow knit shirt. Shay scowled. She distinctly remembered that Ginger had worn a rust-colored shirt to school that day. Had she gone home to change so she would be dressed in the same colors Towe was wearing? Shay watched them together, noticing the way Ginger's copper-colored hair and Towe's red hair seemed to complement each other.

"Mind if I join you?"

Shay looked up quickly as Eric Chapin, braced on crutches, hesitated beside her booth. His sharp features had an unfinished look, like a piece of hand-painted porcelain that still needed a final firing, but his smile was broad and friendly, and Shay smiled back at him.

"Hi, Eric. Sit down. But watch those crutches. They could get broken in the stampede when the music stops."

"Thanks for the warning." Eric dropped down on the bench across the table from her and tucked his crutches out of the way. "You don't look as if you're having a whole bunch of fun."

"I'm with Towe Williams." She blurted the words as if they explained everything; then immediately she wished she had said something else. Anything else.

"The tall guy with the red hair, huh?"

Shay nodded.

"Then what's he doing out there while you're sitting here?"

"Everyone changed partners a while ago, and I was a dropout."

"Don't blame you. Okay if I play dropout with you?"

"Do you like to dance?"

"Sure. Sometimes." He looked at the tabletop. "Well, to be honest, I don't care for dancing all that much. Horses are more my thing. Horses can take up a lot of a guy's time."

"I know. I really do. When I first moved to Tulsa last fall, I didn't know anyone, and I had a lot of extra time. Dancer was my best friend for several months."

He grinned at her again, and she noticed his tip-tilted smile, higher on the left side than on the right. Who was it that said a smile was the most important thing a person could wear? Probably her mother, she thought. She had probably said it when Shay was wanting new clothes.

"Cherokee's still my best friend," Eric said.

"Well, stick around," Shay invited. "I'll introduce you to some of the gang."

"Any of them like to ride?"

"A few do, but not to the extent that they're into showing in the ring."

"Yeah, I know how it is. A person really has to be a dedicated horseman to be interested in getting a horse ready to show. I've only been showing for a year or so. How about you?"

"I entered some shows back east, but I'm just learning western ways. But I guess I'm on vacation for the moment, at least as far as Dancer is concerned."

"You might use the time to teach her tricks," Eric said.

"What kind of tricks? And what for?"

"For fun, mostly. It would just be something to do while you can't ride her."

"Does Cherokee do tricks?"

"Just one. I taught him to bow, to go down on his front knees. I thought it might be fun to have him do it sometime after he's been presented with a trophy."

"How did you train him to do it? It must have taken months."

"No way. It took about an hour, but I never could have done it without that cavalry friend I was telling you about. He taught me the real secret of horse training."

Shay laughed as she looked into Eric's green eyes. "You mean, there's just one secret? One open sesame?"

"That's about it. You have to learn to think like a horse. Once you do that, the rest isn't as hard as it seems."

Shay ordered another cola when the waitress came to take Eric's order; then she leaned forward so she could hear him better. "Give, Eric. How did you learn to think like a horse?"

"I hate shouting," Eric said. "How about going out by the ice-cream bar where it's quieter?"

For an instant Shay was tempted to tell him she couldn't, that she had to wait for Towe; then she thought how ridiculous that would sound. Why should she wait for a guy who was so busy dancing with other girls that he hadn't even stopped by their booth to check on her?

"Yeah, let's do go where it's not so noisy." It'll serve Towe right, she thought. Let him worry a little. Then she frowned. What if he didn't even miss her?

She held Eric's crutches while he pulled himself to his feet, and they went back to the front of the D&D and settled in a booth near the door.

"Okay, give." Shay grinned at him. "Just how does a person start thinking like a horse?"

Eric sipped his drink, then set it aside. "First you ask yourself what a horse wants more than anything else."

Shay thought about that. "A reward? Kind words? A pat on the withers?"

"Your first answer was right. A horse wants a reward. But you're off in left field if you think he's wanting kind words or loving pats."

"Okay, so what does he want?" Shay grinned as she thought of how much Eric reminded her of Molly. The big difference was that Mollie tried to psych out people, but Eric psyched out horses.

"The thing a horse wants most is to be left alone," Eric said.

Shay crunched a piece of ice as she considered that idea.

"You don't believe?" he asked.

"I don't know. Are you saying you taught Cherokee to bow by leaving him alone?"

"You got it."

"Then I don't believe. Sorry."

"The old man helped me. We tied a lead rope around Cherokee's forefeet and tightened it just a bit. Cherokee bowed about an inch as he struggled to free himself. I said 'Good boy' and released the rope. Then I waited ten minutes or so before I repeated the lesson. The next time we tightened the rope, he went down two or three inches. Again I said 'Good boy,' and this time I patted him and released the rope. Get it?"

Shay began to smile. "He wanted to be left alone, right? When you released the rope around his legs, he considered that his reward."

"Right. Within the hour I had taught him to bow to the ground for the reward of being let alone until the next day. Now he'll do it in response to a nudge and a word signal."

Eric impressed Shay with his friendliness and his willingness to share his knowledge. She wanted to ask him more questions, but she saw Towe coming their way. She felt herself tense, felt a pulse beating in her left temple. She smiled at Towe, and when he reached the booth she spoke.

"Towe, this is Eric Chapin. He boards his horse at Redhill Ranch, and he was just telling me about some of his training techniques."

"Do they usually result in a sprained ankle?" Towe glanced at the crutches, then smiled at Eric as he dropped down in the booth beside Shay.

"Not always," Eric said. "Just sometimes."

Shay felt her hand sweating as Towe reached for it,

twining his fingers through hers. What had she expected? Had she expected him to make a scene because she was sitting with another boy? Towe was hardly the kind to start a ruckus with a guy on crutches.

"Ready to dance a few numbers?" Towe asked her.

Shay glanced at her watch. "Really think I'd better be going home, Towe."

"I'm ready if you are." He stood and waited for her to slide from the booth.

"Nice to see you, Eric," Shay said. "And thanks for the training tips."

"See ya around, buddy," Towe called over his shoulder to Eric as he and Shay left the D&D.

They walked home through the golden afternoon sunshine hardly speaking, and Shay's mind was so full of questions and insecure feelings that she thought she couldn't bear their silence. Towe hadn't seemed the least bit jealous of Eric. Yet why should he have shown such feelings? She had hidden her feelings about his dancing with Ginger, hadn't she? What was wrong between them? She wished she had the courage to ask, but she didn't.

When they reached her house, she smiled up at Towe. "Want to come in for a sec? Still got some of those cookies."

"Another time, okay? Got to get home and hit the books."

"Yeah, I've got homework, too." She stepped inside and turned, thinking he might change his mind about coming in, but he was already stepping off the porch.

"See ya, Shay."

Shay went on inside, put her books on her desk, changed clothes. She managed to hold up her end of the dinner-table conversation that evening, but it was an effort. When her folks asked what had happened that day at school, she could think of nothing of interest. All she could think of was Towe dancing with Ginger Netherton, who obviously had gone home and changed into a shirt that matched Towe's. She couldn't talk to her parents about things like that. They wouldn't understand. They wouldn't understand that there was no way she could compete with a girl like Ginger.

"Didn't you have some sort of reading test today?" her mother asked.

"Oh, yeah. We did. Just routine, though. The state is still trying to figure out why Johnny can't read. Personally I think Johnny can read. The state's just doing busywork."

"It's a little late for the whys at the high-school level," her dad said. "By that time they should be figuring out what to do about it."

Shay let the conversation flow around her, and when at last she was able to escape into her room, she pulled the telephone to her bed and dialed Mollie. After pouring her troubles into Mollie's willing ear, she was surprised that her friend wasn't more sympathetic.

"So what's the big deal?" Mollie asked. "Chip and I change partners a lot. Most of the kids do, you know."

"That's not the point," Shay insisted. "Towe and I usually dance together. This afternoon's the first time either of us has danced with another partner when we've been together."

"Was it so terrible?"

"That's not the point," Shay insisted, knowing she was sounding like a broken record.

"Then what *is* the point?"

"It's just that, well, I think we're drifting apart, and I don't want that to happen."

"It was bound to happen sooner or later."

"Mollie, you're supposed to be helping me, not agreeing that yes, Towe and I are drifting apart. I thought maybe you could help."

"How? By telling you how to put the evil eye on Ginger?"

"I don't intend to put the evil eye on anyone. Gol, Mollie, maybe we should hang it up and talk another time. I feel rotten, and you're making me feel worse."

"I'm sorry, Shay. But it's hard for me to offer any advice when I've never been where you're coming from. I've never had a chance to go steady. Nobody's ever been that interested. So how can I help you?"

"I don't know. Maybe nobody can help me."

"Nobody but yourself. You're responsible for you, Shay. If Towe's that important to you, you'll figure out a way to hang on to him. Ginger Netherton's a nerd. A blabbermouth."

"Yeah, a nerd who has a closet full of neat clothes. A nerd who has hair the color of money. A nerd who always knows the right thing to say to a guy. I wish I were that kind of a nerd."

"Don't let her get to you."

"She's already gotten to me. And to Towe."

"Maybe he didn't like to see you sitting there with that new guy. When did you two get so chummy?"

"His name's Eric. Remember? And I didn't think we were all that chummy."

"I was watching you, Shay. You were leaning toward him and hanging on to his words and looking at him as if he were a chocolate brownie and you hadn't had dessert.''

"We were talking about training horses. And if I was leaning toward him, it was because the music was so loud I couldn't hear what he was saying.''

"You needn't be so defensive. He's probably a neat guy. Maybe you've got an inside track with him. Most girls aren't all that crazy about training horses.''

"I wasn't trying for an inside track with him, or any other kind of track. Mollie, are you trying to distract me?''

"Of course not.''

"You are too. But it won't work. Towe's the only guy I'm interested in. He understands me. I can talk to him about almost anything. He's the only guy I ever met that I really want to be with forever.''

"You looked very comfortable with Eric.''

"I wish you'd forget Eric and think about Towe.''

"You seem to be thinking about him enough for both of us. So what if he danced for a while with Ginger? You were talking with Eric, so he danced with another girl. Seems fair enough, doesn't it? I don't blame Towe for being a little jealous. Or maybe that's what you intended.''

"No way.''

"Subconsciously, of course. People do a lot of things for reasons they don't even realize. I'm not blaming you, understand. If I thought there was anything I could do that would make Chip a little green, I wouldn't be above trying it.''

Shay pounded her pillow and scrunched into a more comfortable position. "Mol, I've got news for you. If

Towe was supposed to be jealous of Eric, he didn't get the message. Not at all."

"Maybe he was just pretending. Sometimes guys like to act nonchalant."

"Believe me. He wasn't jealous. And when we got home, he didn't come inside for a few minutes the way he usually does."

"Shay, let me think about this until tomorrow. Sometimes if I sleep on a problem it sort of works itself out in my mind. You might try that, too; then we can talk about it tomorrow before school, okay?"

"Okay." Shay knew Mollie would keep her word. She would think about Towe and Ginger, and maybe she would have an idea tomorrow. But she wanted to end their conversation on a brighter note. "Hey, Mol, I almost forgot to tell you! Dr. Richards says that Dancer may have twins. How about that!"

"Wow! Very nice! That's something to write home about."

"But I can't ride her in the shows."

"Oh."

"But it'll be worth it to have two foals."

"Hey, do me a favor, okay?"

"Sure. What?"

"Write Randy and tell him the details. How about it?"

"Think he'd really be interested?" Shay sat up, ready to bring the conversation to an end.

"Sure he'd be interested. Having firsthand info on a deal like that might get him some brownie points with his professors."

"Yeah, well, I'll see. Thanks for listening, Mollie."

"See ya tomorrow, Shay. Glad you called."

7

After she returned the phone to the hall, Shay considered writing to Randy. She didn't doubt that he would be interested in Dancer and in Dr. Richard's assessment of her condition. Randy had asked her to write him, hadn't he? She went to her desk and got out her stationery, but she sat staring at it, unable to get started.

Dear Randy,
   I've just been talking to Mollie and

What was the matter with her? She knew Randy would be interested in Dancer. She sighed. Maybe that was the problem. Randy would be more interested in Dancer than he would be in her. But so what? Why did she think she had to be first with everyone? She expected Mollie to listen to her with an understanding heart. She expected Towe to be at her beck and call. She expected . . . well, maybe she expected too much of everyone.

She picked up her ball-point again and finished the letter to Randy. If the information would help him, fine. If he cared to answer the letter, fine. She studied for a while and then she went to bed; but when she closed her eyes, she saw mental images of Towe dancing with Ginger, images of Ginger gazing up at him and smiling in that I've-got-a-secret way of hers.

The next morning Mollie had no solution to the Ginger Netherton problem, and Shay's solution was to concentrate on math and English and history, and to allow her mind no time to wander to thoughts of Towe and Ginger. And it worked. At least she got through the morning.

Towe met her at the water fountain as usual, and they walked to the cafeteria together for lunch. Ginger was sitting with her ususal group of in people, giving her special smile to the captain of the basketball team.

"Going out to ride this afternoon?" Towe asked.

Shay swallowed the last of an apple as she shook her head. "Can't ride, but I'm going out to give Dancer a grooming. A lady expecting twins should be pampered, don't you think?"

"By all means."

"Are you going out to ride? We could tandem on King, I suppose." Even before the words were completely out, she wished she hadn't asked. She knew Towe was going to refuse by the way he was looking at the floor and sort of kicking at the leg of her chair.

"Have to help Dad at the shop today," Towe said. "He thinks I should learn about brake linings, so that's going to be the lesson of the afternoon."

"Sounds fascinating," Shay said, wondering if the brake-lining lesson would be like the car-waxing session, very short if not nonexistent.

"Want to come watch?"

"Thanks, but no, thanks." She knew Towe was kidding about watching. Having a girl hanging around the shop was one of his father's no-nos. And she was glad. It would be really hard to act interested in a brake lining.

Towe walked with her to her locker while she got her books for afternoon classes; then he walked with her to the civics classroom. She knew that made him have to hurry to reach his own second-floor chemistry room before the tardy bell rang. But it was their established routine. She was pleased with it. There was a lot of comfort in routine.

Afternoon classes passed as usual, and Shay didn't expect Towe to meet her after school, since he was going to work. She hurried home, changed clothes, and rode her bike to the stable. For a moment she was surprised to see that Eric was already there; then she remembered that he had the use of his dad's truck. She smiled to herself. There were some advantages to having a bad leg. Eric always had wheels.

"Hi," Eric called to her. "I hoped you'd be out here today."

"You did? Can I help you with Cherokee?"

"Would you mind helping me get him from the pasture? He'll come when he sees me, but I have a problem with opening and closing the gate."

"Sure. No sweat."

Shay slowed her pace to match Eric's lurching stride, and they walked toward the pasture. Every day the grass seemed greener, more lush, than it had the day before. But Towe had said it wouldn't last. He said that during the hot months the pasture would turn brown, or at least almost brown. It was hard to imagine such a thing on a day like this one.

A meadowlark sang from a rocky outcropping near the

creek, and a redheaded woodpecker drummed on a hollow oak. Overhead, a hawk glided on an updraft, looking more like a kite than a living bird. Shay breathed in the fresh fragrance of the sun-warmed grass, the sweet-pungent smell of the stream, and she felt sorry for Towe, cooped up in a garage with a faulty brake lining.

Even before she whistled for Dancer, the mare saw her and trotted toward the gate. Eric whistled for Cherokee. At first the gelding pretended not to hear; then gradually he began walking toward the stable. When he saw Dancer trotting, his competitive spirit came to life; they raced toward the fence, snorting and stamping as their noses touched the gate.

"If you'll open the gate, I can grab his halter," Eric said.

Shay obliged, snapped Dancer's lead rope to her halter, then closed the gate behind them. Again she walked slowly with Eric as they led the horses to the hitching rail.

"Not much fun grooming a horse you can't ride," Eric said. "But I don't want Cherokee to forget who's boss."

"Yeah, right. Both of us have really had our plans for the summer changed, haven't we? Of course, you'll be off those crutches before long."

They brushed and combed the horses in silence for a few minutes. Then Eric spoke.

"Would you like to saddle Cherokee and ride him a little? I won't mind. It'd do him good."

"And it would do me good, too." Shay laughed. "I miss being able to ride whenever I please."

When they had finished the grooming, Shay saddled Cherokee and rode him around the arena, changing gaits as Eric called them. When she stopped at the fence where Eric was standing, she smiled down at him. "He's really okay, Eric. He responds at the slightest signal."

"Shay?" Eric hesitated a moment, then glanced into the distance before he looked back at her. "Would you like to ride Cherokee for me in the first Saddle Club show? I mean, since you have no horse, and since my horse has no rider, maybe we could work out something just this once."

"You mean you wouldn't mind?"

"Of course I'd mind, but let's face it. It would be good for both of us. I've watched you. You handle Cherokee well from the ground. And you're a good rider, too. I wouldn't make such an offer to just anyone."

Shay felt her heart racing, but she held back a definite reply. "Let me think about it, Eric. Let me think about it and talk it over with my folks, okay?"

"If you win a trophy, you can keep it," Eric said. "That would only be fair, and it would give you a chance to win the right to represent the club at the state fair in the fall."

"I'll let you know tomorrow, okay?"

"Deal."

Shay unsaddled Cherokee and helped Eric brush him down again. Then they both stood back and watched the gelding roll in the dust.

"Some good that grooming did!" Shay laughed and stood back to avoid flying dust as Cherokee rose to his feet and shook himself.

"Horses are just like little kids. Get them cleaned up and they can't wait to get dirty again. Can I give you a lift home?"

"Thanks, Eric, but I'm not going just yet."

"Okay, see ya around tomorrow."

"Right."

Shay watched Eric's truck leave a slipstream of dust behind it as he drove down the dirt road to the blacktop. Why hadn't she gone with him? She knew why. She didn't want anyone to see her with Eric and report the news to Towe. And what was she going to do about riding Cherokee in the first show? All her instincts told her to grab the chance, but she would talk it over with her folks. It never hurt to have a second opinion.

When she pedaled into her driveway, Shay was surprised to see Towe's car approaching her house from the other direction.

"Hi," she called to him as he stopped at the curbing. "Finish with the brake lining early?"

"Yeah, it's all finished. Dad had to start it before I got there."

"Why didn't you bike on out to the stable? Come on in and I'll get us a cola."

Towe got out of his car, and they walked her bike to the garage before they went inside. He sat down at the kitchen table as he had done dozens of other times, yet Shay sensed that something was wrong. She washed her hands, placed ice cubes in glasses, poured Coke over them. She had hardly sat down across from Towe before he came right to the point of his visit.

"Shay, there's something I've been wanting to talk with you about."

She felt her heart fluttering inside her chest. Yesterday, last week, she might have thought he was going to ask her to wear his class ring. But not today. She braced herself.

"What is it, Towe?"

"It's hard for me to say. I don't want to hurt you or anything, but . . ."

"But?" But you'd rather go with Ginger Netherton? But you'd rather I got lost? But you'd rather never see me again? She could think of a lot of lines to follow his hesitation.

"I think we should cool our relationship a little, Shay."

"Oh." His words had sounded practiced, rehearsed, but she could think of nothing to say.

"I don't want to break up, but I think we both need a little more space to operate in."

"Oh."

"I still want to go out with you, and I hope you still want to go out with me, but couldn't we make it a little less exclusive? I mean, I think we should continue dating but also go out with others, too. What do you think?"

Shay's tongue suddenly felt so stiff she knew she couldn't speak. Yet she had to say something, and she had to say it quickly or her silence would reveal more of her inner feelings than she was willing to share with Towe at the moment.

"Maybe it would be a good idea, Towe. I certainly don't want to hold you to any promises you don't want to keep."

"Hold on a minute, Shay. It's not that I don't want to keep my promise. It's just . . . well, I told you. I think we need more room to operate."

All at once Shay wanted to giggle hysterically. *Room to operate.* She could imagine Towe in an operating room in mask and surgical coat. He was about to remove her heart.

"If that's what you want, then that's what I want, too, Towe." Maybe, if they cooled it a bit, he would miss her. Maybe he would be eager enough to go out with her again. She sighed. That was a bunch of wishful thinking. She couldn't imagine that absence from her would make his heart grow fonder, unless maybe it grew fonder of Ginger Netherton.

"I'm just saying let's try it and see how it goes." Towe scuffed his toe against the leg of the drop-leaf table. "Let's date each other, but let's also date others for a month or so. Then we can see how we feel about each other."

"Fair enough." Shay watched condensation run down the outside of her cola glass like cold tears. What else was there to say?

"I'll call you again after I've had a date with someone else, and after you've been out with someone else. Okay? We'll sort of talk things over then and see how we feel."

"Okay."

She was glad when Towe stood and left the kitchen and the house without lingering to talk more about their dating. How unfair of him. It would be easy for him to find another girl. All he had to do was to ask. But what about her? She wasn't about to approach some other boy. No way. What if she asked someone out and he said no? And who could she expect to ask her out? She was tagged as Towe's girl, and it would take a while for the message to get around to the boys that she and Towe were free-lancing.

And once the word did get around, she doubted if anyone would call her. It would look as if Towe had dropped her, wouldn't it? Shay felt tears brimming, and she ran to her room and closed the door before her parents came in and asked what was wrong.

Didn't Mollie always say it was good for a person to cry when she felt like crying? Well, she felt like it right now, that's for sure. She buried her head in her pillow for a few seconds. Then she sat up. No! She wasn't going to cry. Tears would only distract her. She needed to think, to plan a course of action.

She bathed her face in cold water, fluffed some powder on her nose and chin. She didn't want her folks to come in and find her teary-eyed, nor did she want to discuss Towe with them. She knew they would try to console her, that they would have advice for her; but no matter what they said or did, she also knew they couldn't possibly understand how awful she felt. She couldn't talk about Towe to someone who didn't understand.

It was her mother's turn to get dinner, and Shay didn't go to the kitchen until she was called.

"Your favorite tonight, Shay, chicken salad with pineapple."

"Great, Mom. How was your day?"

"The usual. Lots of people going through the pottery showroom this afternoon. Maybe vacation season is starting early this year. Older people these were, of course. Mostly women. Not many men or kids."

"Is the company still going to rearrange the show-room?" Shay tried to keep the conversation focused on her mother and her activities.

"Yes, but not until June. A while yet. It might be that you could get a job out there for a few days during the changing, if you're interested."

"I'll see. Maybe I should apply for it."

When her father came in from the hospital, they all sat down to eat. "Haven't seen Towe around lately, Shay. I suppose the seniors are really busy getting ready for graduation."

"I suppose so." She thought she might scream if her father kept on talking about Towe.

"The car's been sounding sort of funny lately. Thought I'd ask Towe to take a listen, see what he thought."

"He was here a few minutes ago, but he's not coming back tonight. Maybe you should just take the car in and let his dad take a look at it."

"Yeah, I suppose so. Just thought it would be a good experience for Towe to try to diagnose the problem. I'd pay him, of course."

"Anything new at school?" her mother asked.

"Not at school, but there's something new at the ranch that I need to ask you about."

"I suppose they've raised their boarding prices." Her father sighed.

"No, Dad. At least, not yet. It's about riding in the show coming up. Eric Chapin has offered to let me ride his gelding. You know Eric—the boy with the sprained ankle."

"Oh." Her mother nodded. "That's really nice of him. What did you tell him?"

"I told him we'd talk it over. Do you think it would be all right?"

"Don't see why not," her father said. "It'd be a good deal for both of you. He gets experience for his horse, and you get to enter the show as you'd planned to do."

"Can you handle his horse, Shay?" her mother asked.

"Yes. I rode him this afternoon. He responds well to my signals."

"Eric evidently likes the way you handle his horse, or he wouldn't have offered to let you ride him," her father said. "I'd go with it if I were you."

It was settled, and Shay was glad. She was glad she would have a horse to ride and glad that the conversation about it had taken up the rest of the dinner hour, leaving no more time for any more talk about Towe.

After dinner Mollie called Shay before Shay had had a chance to dial her number. "Hey, Shay! What's this I hear about you and Towe breaking up?"

For a moment Shay was stunned. How could the word have gotten around so soon? She pulled the telephone into her room and closed the door. "Who told you that?"

"It seems that Towe told Ginger, and you know Ginger. Telling her anything is the same as broadcasting it. The second she found out, she asked Towe to the turnabout mixer on Friday night. Give, Shay, is all this true?"

"Well, it's not quite true that we've broken up. We've just decided to cool it a little, to keep on dating, but to date others, too."

"Sounds like a sensible plan to me."

"I thought it would."

"Meaning you hate the whole idea, right?"

"Something like that. It really bugs me that Towe ran right to Ginger with the news."

"Not very subtle of him. But at least he warned you first. You have the same privilege, don't you?"

Shay listened to the telephone hum for a few seconds; then she blurted her true feelings. "What am I going to *do*, Mollie? How can I face school tomorrow? Everyone will be talking and whispering behind my back."

"Why don't you latch on to Eric? That'd make everyone wonder whose idea the breakup was."

"We're not breaking up!"

"Sorry. That'd make everyone wonder whose idea it was to cool the relationship. That any better?"

"Much. But you needn't think I'm going to latch on to anyone just for the looks of it." Shay said the words, but deep down she wished there were someone she could latch on to. She hadn't realized how much she had grown to depend on Towe. She expected him to be there when she needed him. And now he wasn't going to be.

"You wouldn't be latching on to Eric just for the looks of it," Mollie said. "There's this girl-ask-boy mixer thing coming up Friday. You could ask Eric to that. I've already asked Chip."

"What did he say?"

"He said yes. What did you expect him to say?"

"Yes." Shay sighed. "I don't know, Mol. It's different with you and Chip. You've been dating off and on for a long time. I just don't like the idea of asking Eric when we've never been out together before."

"Girls ask boys out every day, Shay. Get with it."

"I just wouldn't know how to approach him. All he's ever talked to me about is horses."

"You can't expect him to try to date a girl who's going steady, you know."

"Maybe I should ask Towe. We're not going to break off entirely."

"I tell you, Ginger's already asked him. And the word I get is that he accepted. Do yourself a favor and ask Eric. Give old Towe something to think about—something except Ginger, that is."

"Wash your mouth out with soap, Mollie. You're talking dirty." Shay tried for a light touch, but she knew she wasn't fooling Mollie. Mollie knew her well enough to guess the truth, to guess that her heart was shattered. But at least Mollie let her hang on to her self-respect by suggesting that she thought Eric would be glad to go out with her.

"See ya at school tomorrow, Shay. Hang in there. Want me to stop by for you?"

"Yeah. Wish you would."

"Okay. Be ready."

After she hung up, Shay thought about what a good friend Mollie was. Mollie had known it would be hard for Shay to go to school alone. Would Towe hang around Ginger in the halls? Or would he walk Shay to her classes as he usually did? She guessed she wouldn't be seeing much of Towe in the halls. Only the steadies walked together to every class.

The next day at school was the pits, in spite of all Mollie's well-intentioned help. As far as Shay was concerned, Towe might have disappeared from the face of the earth. She opened her own locker, carried her own books, got to her classes without being escorted. All through lunch hour she talked to Mollie and Chip to keep herself from looking around the cafeteria to see what Towe was doing.

Afternoon classes dragged. When Miss Johnson assigned an English theme to be completed by the following Monday, Shay sighed to herself. She had always liked Miss Johnson, who was friendly and helpful. And she admired her because sometimes she wrote poems which were published in the *Tulsa World*. But why was she doing this to them right at the end of school?

"I want you to describe your life ten years from now," Miss Johnson said.

Everyone groaned.

"Look to nature for your ideas," Miss Johnson said.

"How?" Mollie asked.

"Look at the green springtime all around you," Miss Johnson said. "Pretend you're a green leaf."

Everyone laughed.

"I'm serious," Miss Johnson said. "The leaves are full of green chlorophyll now, but beautiful colors are hidden under all that green. As the leaves mature in the fall, other colors will show through."

"But we're not leaves," Chip called out.

Miss Johnson smiled. "I think you are like leaves in some ways, Chip. I think that, if you try, you can look through your own greenness and find your true colors, the colors that will begin to distinguish you as you become mature people."

Everyone groaned again.

"I can't do it, Mollie," Shay said after class that afternoon. "I haven't any idea what I'll be doing ten years from now."

"I do." Mollie smiled. "I mean, I have an idea about what I'll be doing, not what you'll be doing. Let's go to the D&D and talk about it."

"Okay." Shay sighed. At least she still had Mollie. And the D&D.

"Bring a notebook. We may want to make some notes."

Obediently Shay pulled her notebook from her locker. But why? She knew she wouldn't have any ideas. She was just letting Mollie boss her around the way Towe always did. She scowled. Why had she thought that about Mollie, about Towe? Towe hadn't bossed her around. She had always wanted to do whatever he wanted to do. She had always wanted to please him.

At the D&D the smell of chocolate was so sweetly strong that they both ordered sodas, and they gave them their full attention before they opened their notebooks and began talking about the theme.

"Just what do you think you'll be doing in ten years?" Shay asked.

"Well, let's start with the basic facts. In ten years we'll both be about twenty-eight years old."

"Gosh, that's old enough to have gone to college, to be married, to have started a family."

"Yeah. But first we have to finish high school. Next year I'm going to really hit the books on the college prep courses. Maybe I'll go to school at Oral Roberts U. It goes in for whole-person education. I believe in that approach to psychology, to anything."

Shay didn't bother to ask Mollie to elaborate on that idea. She was just trying to think of something she could write about that would please Miss Johnson.

"College? I'm not really sure I even want to go to college, Mollie. I think about it, but I just don't know."

"It isn't required, you know. It's just what I happen to want to do. You have to have lots of education to be a good psychologist."

"I just thought maybe I'd get married."

"Right out of high school?"

Shay nodded. "Why not? If a person plans to raise a family, then why bother with college? My mother married Dad when she was eighteen, and she's happy."

"Who do you plan to marry?"

Shay studied the melted chocolate on the inside of her soda glass. It surprised her to realize that deep down in her thinking she had planned to marry Towe. But she couldn't say that. Not even to Mollie. She and Towe had never talked of marriage. They had never even talked about her wearing his class ring! But in her mind and her heart she had felt that marriage was the career for her. And she knew Towe was the boy for her.

"I don't know who I plan to marry, Mollie. But I could write that I plan for marriage to be my thing. Women's lib doesn't mean that every woman has to have a career. It means that every woman can choose what she's going to do with her life."

"Right. But with prices skyrocketing, lots of women have to go to work just to help hold their families together. At least, that's what my mom says. She's started working at Harwelden for the Arts and Humanities Council."

"I didn't know that. When did she start?"

"Last week."

"How come you didn't say anything about it?"

"You never asked."

"Mollie!"

"Okay, okay. I never said anything because I don't like it very much, I guess."

"Little girl wants Mommy home when she gets in from school?" Shay teased.

"No, that's not it. I was going to talk to you about it the other night, but we just never got around to it."

Shay remembered Mollie's saying that she needed a listening ear, and she felt ashamed that she hadn't asked Mollie about it at the time. But Randy had been with them. And other things had come up in her own life.

"Mollie, what's with this job of your mother's? I mean, is your family in financial trouble? Big trouble or something?"

"No." Mollie closed her notebook. "It's just that we have extra bills. And it's just that Mom's almost forty-five and she's never had any business experience."

"She's smart. She'll catch on."

"Yeah, but at Harwelden she's just a file clerk. The pay is minimum wage. It's for the birds. Mom's worth more than that—a lot more."

"Is she complaining?"

"No, she's not the complaining type."

"Maybe something better will come along for her."

"It's not likely to, Shay. Mom needs more education. Of course, I'll be helping out this summer as soon as I find a job, but I'll just get minimum wage, too. I think any girl is crazy who doesn't prepare for some sort of well-paying job. Marriage is fine and dandy, but the day may come when a second paycheck will be a necessity."

"I suppose you're right, but I don't know what I'd prepare for." Shay chewed on the end of her pencil. Her dream had included Towe, and that was about as far as it had gone. She could imagine Towe coming home to her each evening. She could imagine their house. She could even imagine some children, a boy for him, a girl for her. When she thought about the dream seriously, it seemed sort of corny, like the words from an old-fashioned song. She had used Towe as a mirror, seeing herself reflected in his eyes, letting him tell her who she was. And now the mirror was gone.

"I thought you were interested in being a veterinarian. Or was that just a line you were handing out to Randy?"

"I don't hand out lines, Mol. You know me better than that, don't you?"

"Okay, so you were sort of thinking about studying to be a vet. Why don't you pick up on that? At least for the English assignment. Miss Johnson's just trying to make us think a little. It's really sort of fun."

"I guess it could be, at that. Mollie, what do you really think you'll be doing ten years from now? What kind of work? Who will your husband be? What kind of work will he be doing?"

Mollie tilted her head to one side and gazed at the ceiling as if in deep thought. "Well, I've always dreamed of being a psychologist, and that includes living in a big house with a pool and a tennis court."

"And I'd like a live-in maid and cook, and an eight-bedroom house with a terrific view of the sea. And I'd like a spaceship for long trips and a helicopter just for short hops to the grocery store."

"Dream on, Shay, dream on."

They ended their session at the D&D with gales of laughter as their imaginary lives in the next decade grew more and more fanciful.

"Maybe the theme will be fun to write, at that," Shay said. "Miss Johnson has a good sense of humor." Then she grew sober. "You know, Mol, what she's really asking us to do is to think about what we want from life."

"Yeah. And aren't we lucky? Really, I mean? We've got so much to choose from, so many ideas to explore."

They had gathered their books and were just leaving their booth when the door to the D&D opened and Ginger stepped inside, followed by Towe. Shay wished she could disappear, but she held her head high, smiled, and nodded a greeting. Then she stepped outside with Mollie.

"Tough," Mollie said. "Really tough, but you handled it well. A smile. An aloof nod. I couldn't have done better myself. If there's anything a guy can't stand, it's a girl who comes unglued in public."

Shay told Mollie goodbye and walked on toward home. Her mind was a turmoil of worry about Towe and Ginger, about the English theme due on Monday. For a while, when she had been laughing with Mollie about it, the theme had seemed to be an easy assignment. But now the laughs were all gone. And if she were to be honest in the theme she would have to say that what she wanted from life was Towe Williams. It was as simple as that. But she certainly couldn't write that in an English theme. No way.

8

The next day at school Shay tried not to mind when Towe didn't appear to escort her to her classes. She walked down the corridors with her head high, but from the corner of her eye she watched to see if Towe was walking with Ginger. He wasn't. At least not yet. At lunch Mollie told Shay that the rumor about Ginger and Towe going together to the Friday-night mixer was all over the whole school.

"What am I going to do, Mollie?" Shay asked. "If it had been any other girl except Ginger, it wouldn't be quite so bad." But in her heart she knew she would have felt the same way no matter who Towe had chosen to free-lance with.

"Why don't you ask Eric to the mixer?" Mollie suggested again. "At least that would be putting a happy face on a bad deal. And if both you and Towe show up with different partners, it would look . . . well, it would look better somehow."

"How can I ask Eric to a dance? He's on crutches."

"I'm on the dance committee, and we're hunting

someone to be in charge of the music. It's hard to find someone to do that. You know, choose and change the records, keep the turntable spinning. It's a no-fun job for the kids who want to dance, but with you and Eric it would be different. Think about it, okay?''

"Some fun." Shay finished her milk and bit into an apple.

"It might not be as much fun as dancing, but you've got to remember that Eric won't be on crutches forever."

"And when he's on both feet again, he'll be ever grateful to me for befriending him in his hour of need?"

"Something like that." Mollie offered Shay a lemon drop.

"I won't count on it."

"Suit yourself. But if you decide to ask him, you can double with Chip and me. I'm driving. I think the role reversal is going to make it a fun party."

Somehow the school day ended, and as Shay was standing in front of her locker she sensed someone hovering behind her. Towe? Her heart leaped into her throat. She had never believed that was possible before, but now she knew that her heart was actually right there next to her tonsils somewhere and she could hardly swallow. She stalled as if searching for something until she thought she could manage to face Towe. When she turned, Eric was grinning at her.

"What's the decision, Shay? You want to ride Cherokee in the show?"

Shay smiled up at Eric and nodded as she slammed her locker door and snapped the lock. "If the offer's still open, I'm going to grab it."

"Great! If you're going to the ranch this afternoon, I'll be glad to share my wheels."

"I've got to stop by home first and change into riding clothes, then I'm going out to see Dancer."

"I'll wait for you. Let's go with it."

Shay matched her pace to Eric's as he swung down the hall on his crutches. Was anyone noticing? Was anyone whispering that Shay Stuart had a new boyfriend? Of course it wasn't true, but the rumor might get started, and that kind of rumor didn't hurt a girl at all. She liked the faint scent of neat's-foot oil that clung to Eric's clothes. Somehow it seemed like a cleaner smell than gasoline.

Eric waited in his truck while Shay changed into riding jeans and boots, and when they drove to Redhill Ranch, Shay thought the spring sunshine had never been brighter, the sky never more blue. Eric drove slowly, and as they approached the ranch they saw Cherokee calmly grazing in the pasture.

"Watch this, Shay." Eric smiled at her, then stuck his head from the truck window and gave a shrill whistle.

Shay watched Cherokee suddenly come to life. His head came up. His ears pricked forward. "He's beautiful, Eric!"

"Look at him go." Eric kept his gaze on the gelding as he burst into a prancing trot, following the truck along the pasture fenceline with his nostrils flaring, his tail high.

"What style! He acts as if he owns the world!" Shay kept her eyes on the horse.

"That's the way I like him to look in the show arena. Fully collected."

"But how do you get him to look that way in the ring? Right now he's excited at seeing you, but in the ring there won't be that incentive."

"I don't try to keep him excited," Eric said. "That'll only make him nervous. And using physical force will make him dull and mechanical in his paces, so I never use that method. I just work for balance."

"Balance." Shay repeated the word as if she had never heard it before. "You're trying to tell me something important, aren't you?"

"Nothing you don't already know. I mean, you know it in your bones, if not in your brain. And if you get your bones and your brain working together, Cherokee should win that trophy for you on Saturday."

"Win it for us," Shay corrected.

"Whatever." Eric drove on to the parking area beside the stable and shut off the ignition. When he said nothing more, Shay spoke again.

"There's something I'm not doing to suit you, isn't there?"

"You're the rider, Shay. But if you'd think more about balance, I think you'd enjoy Cherokee a lot more."

"In what way? I mean, what should I do about balance?"

"You can see that a horse is heavier in front than behind. Most of his weight is over his front legs. The hind legs furnish his propulsion. When he collects himself, he shifts his weight to his rear legs."

"And he's ready to use those hind legs for lift and drive, right?"

"Right. So when you're in the ring and you want him

to collect himself, you have to signal him to shift his weight back. Then he can lift himself lightly into a turn, drive forward smoothly, or stop suddenly.''

"What signal do you use?''

"Just a simple knee signal. Both knees. Why don't you give it a try and see what happens? I'm sure he'll respond to you the same way he does to me.''

They saddled Cherokee, and Shay rode him into the arena, listening to the squeak of the stirrups, the swish of Cherokee's tail. As Eric called the signals she was careful not to rush Cherokee into a change of gait or a change of direction. Using the double knee signal, she gave him time to balance himself.

"Neat!'' Eric called from the sidelines where he was leaning on the arena fence. "You both look great.''

Shay kept the work session short, not wanting to tire or bore Cherokee, and when she dismounted at the hitching rail, Eric removed Cherokee's saddle and bridle and began grooming him.

"Want me to help?''

"Don't you want to groom Dancer?''

"Yes, but I'll help you with Cherokee if you want me to.''

"I can manage. You get Dancer. I have to get the truck back home in a half hour or so.''

They worked together at the hitching rail, brushing, combing, not bothering to talk. The silence between them was a pleasant one. Sometimes when she was with Towe, she talked just for the sake of avoiding silence. But not always.

After they had turned both horses back to pasture and they were on their way home, Shay blurted the words that had been in the back of her mind ever since she had talked with Mollie in the lunchroom.

"Eric, there's a spring mixer at school tomorrow night. The girls are supposed to ask the boys. Would you like to go with me?" She watched the way Eric's face turned the color of ripe plums, and for a moment her mouth went as dry as paper. Was he going to turn her down? Was this how boys felt when they asked a girl out? Was there always a nagging fear of rejection?

"I'd like to go with you, Shay. But are you sure you want me to? I mean, with this leg and all, I won't be the life of the party."

"Life-of-the-party types are bummers." Shay grinned at him. "Mollie says the dance committee needs someone to manage the music. We could do that."

"It's a deal." Eric stopped the truck in front of her house. "This won't cause problems between you and Towe, will it?"

"It won't cause any problems. Mollie McNamara has asked me to double with her and Chip Parris. That okay with you? You know Chip, don't you?"

"Yeah, I've met him. And doubling will be fine. I'll really be looking forward to it."

"Me, too, Eric." Shay opened the truck door. "Don't get out. I can manage."

Eric laid his crutch back down. "Thanks. I won't be on these too much longer, I hope."

Shay slammed the truck door, waved at Eric, and hurried on toward her front door. Once she was inside, she turned and waved again as he drove off. It had been that easy! She could hardly believe that she had a date with a boy who wasn't Towe Williams. And she was actually looking forward to it. Or was she just looking forward to proving to the rest of the kids that Towe hadn't jilted her? She called Mollie the minute supper was over and the kitchen was in order, but they didn't talk long. Mollie congratulated her, and Shay began her homework in a relaxed frame of mind.

When she settled down to work on her English theme, she tried to pretend that she really wanted to be a vet. She tried to see herself as a career woman to whom romance and marriage were of secondary importance. But her writing didn't ring true.

The next day, Mollie read Shay's theme and just shook her head. "Scrap it, Shay. You can do better than that. It's stilted and wordy."

She took Mollie's advice and began the theme again. This time she wrote a farce in which she married a famous movie star and moved to Mexico.

Mollie laughed a lot at Shay's theme, but Shay knew that deep inside herself she was refusing to face the realities of her life. Deep inside herself, she still saw Towe Williams as the one important man in her life.

"What are you going to wear to the mixer tonight?" Mollie asked as she and Shay walked home from school that afternoon.

"Jeans." Shay sighed. "Mom said I couldn't buy new ones, so I'm wearing the same old dress jeans with my blue shirt and my white V-neck vest."

"You look great in that outfit. There's one big advantage in not going steady, Shay. At least Eric hasn't seen all your clothes a jillion times already."

"I suppose you're right."

"Of course, I don't have to worry much about

clothes, either. Chip doesn't take me out enough to remember what I wear. At least, I don't think he does.''

"You might be surprised. What are you wearing?''

"My white jeans and a red shirt.''

Shay smiled. Only Mollie could believe that a guy wouldn't remember her screaming red shirts and sweaters. A red shirt was Mollie's trademark.

That night Shay dressed carefully, using greenish eye shadow and lots of mascara to bring out her eyes and adding blusher to give her cheeks a little more life. Did Eric like girls with lots of makeup, or did he prefer girls with a natural look? She realized how little she knew about him. Most of their talk had been of horses. But no matter. She and Towe hadn't broken up. Her next date would surely be with Towe, and she would know exactly how to dress and make up her face. Or would she? Maybe she had been doing something wrong. Maybe that was why Towe wanted a change of scene.

Mollie honked the horn for Shay at seven o'clock and they went to pick up the boys, stopping for Chip first, then Eric. As usual, Chip had on jeans and his Tulsa Ice Oilers shirt with his sax reeds in the pocket, but Eric was wearing brown cord slacks and a tan shirt that looked as if it might be new. Shay smiled to herself as she thought he had as much style as Cherokee. Maybe it was a matter of balance? He certainly had had enough practice balancing on those crutches.

"We're getting there early to be sure the turntable and records are where they're supposed to be,'' Shay said after Eric had settled himself in the car.

"Just play the oldies,'' Chip said. "That's what everyone wants to hear.''

"We'll play everything that's there," Shay promised.

The school gym smelled of stale smoke and popcorn from the last game. It was as noisy as an echo chamber, and it was crowded even though they had arrived early. Shay wanted to rush across the shiny hardwood floor and take her place at the turntable, but there was no rushing Eric and the crutches. She felt as if they were passing in review as they walked to the refreshment table and on to the area behind it that had been reserved as the music center.

"Let's spin one," a voice called out as they sat down beside the turntable. "Let's get this party cracking."

"You've got it," Shay called. And in a moment the gym floor was vibrating to sound from the Bee Gees. Shay watched the crowd as couples began to take the floor. Could it be that Towe wasn't present? She didn't see him.

"You're going to be bored to death," Eric said after three Bee Gees numbers. "If you'd like to dance with someone else, I won't mind."

"No way." Shay smiled at him. "How about some punch and a few cookies?"

"Sounds good."

Shay filled two paper cups with punch, and the red liquid sloshed and threatened to spill as she saw Towe and Ginger enter at the far end of the gym. She handed Eric's punch cup to him and then returned to the refreshment table for cookies. But all the time she was watching Towe and trying to pretend that she wasn't watching him. It didn't matter. He certainly wasn't watching her. He acted as if Ginger might disappear if his gaze left her even for an instant. And Shay really couldn't blame him. Ginger looked so neat. Designer jeans. Rust-colored sweater. Her long coppery hair fanned out over her shoulders.

"Hang in there," Mollie whispered into Shay's ear. "Everybody is asking about your date. They want to know how long you've been going with him, where you met him."

"Thanks for the good words, Mollie, but—"

"But nothing. Live it up. You've got a good deal—a handsome guy on one side and the refreshments on the other. Live!"

Shay carried the cookies back to share with Eric, and she didn't glance in Towe's direction again.

"Bored?" Eric asked.

"No way. Are you?"

"Frankly, yes." Eric blushed. "I mean, not with you, of course. But like I'm certainly bored with being tied down to those crutches. I could go for dancing tonight. Sitting on the sidelines all the time is for the birds, especially when I could be out there on the floor with you."

"Maybe next time," Shay said, secretly glad that Eric at least wanted to dance with her.

At ten o'clock the dance chaperons declared an intermission, and everyone crowded around the refreshment table. Shay grinned and agreed when Eric suggested they leave the gym for a few minutes. The outside air was cool, and moonlight flooded the area behind the gymnasium. They leaned against a retaining wall that overlooked the tennis courts, and Eric took her hand.

"It was neat of you to invite me to this party, Shay. It's tough, moving to a new school, not knowing anyone."

"I know. A few months ago I was new here, too. I remember how I felt so out of it. And a sprained ankle doesn't help any, either, does it?"

"Don't know about that. If it hadn't been for the old ankle, we might not have gotten acquainted."

"Don't tell me you're a look-for-the-silver-lining type." Shay laughed, and when Eric squeezed her hand she returned the squeeze.

"There are silver linings." He looked into her eyes. "You can't deny that. And you're my silver lining for this evening."

Shay eased into the circle of Eric's arm, surprised that it was so easy to talk with him. Of course they had talked easily about horses and riding, but this was something quite different. She liked it.

"Shay?" Mollie's voice carried to her from the gym door. "How about getting the music started again? The natives are getting restless."

"Sure thing!" Shay turned toward the gym, reluctant to leave the warmth of Eric's nearness, the touch of his arm on her shoulder, the feel of his hand in hers. She waited for him to get his crutches from where he had balanced them against the retaining wall and adjust them.

"Duty calls," Eric said with a groan. "Wouldn't you know!"

Shay felt a pleasant sensation deep inside her. Eric had wanted to talk longer. Eric liked her. She hadn't known it could be so easy to be with a boy who wasn't Towe Williams.

Once they were back inside the gym, the air felt stuffy and hot, and now it seemed to hold the smell of gym shoes and sweat socks. The music was too loud, too insistent. Shay wished she were still outside with Eric's arm around her. She was eager for the dance to end, eager for more quiet minutes alone with Eric.

"How nice of you to do all the hard work with the music, Shay."

Shay looked up quickly when she heard Ginger's voice. Was Ginger rubbing it in? Rubbing in the fact that she was with Towe and Shay wasn't?

"It's been fun, Ginger." Shay forced herself to smile and to be polite.

"How about a Springsteen tune?" Towe asked, following Ginger to the turntable.

"Sure, man," Eric said. "Got one right here. We'll put it next in line."

A Springsteen tune. How could Towe be so insensitive! She used to think of Springsteen numbers as *their* special music. Evidently Towe hadn't thought of the tunes that way at all. She pretended to be very busy sorting records until Towe and Ginger stepped back onto the floor and began dancing again.

When at last the evening ended, Mollie drove Eric home first and waited while Shay walked with him to the door.

"You needn't bother going clear to the door," Eric said.

"Oh, but a good escort sees her date safely inside."

When they reached the shadow of Eric's front porch, he turned and reached for her hand again. "Thanks for a neat evening, Shay." He squeezed her hand. "We'll do it again sometime, okay?"

"Okay. I'll be looking forward to it." She found herself holding her breath. If he said "see ya," she thought, she might scream. But he didn't. And she felt that he really meant it when he said they'd get together again sometime, although he hadn't specified the exact time. As she got back into the car with Mollie and Chip she felt confused. She had expected to have a miserable time without Towe, but she had enjoyed the evening with Eric. She had enjoyed it very much.

9

Shay lay awake a long time that night trying to sort out her feelings. That afternoon she had actually ached when she thought of Towe and Ginger together. She had a hard time considering Towe anything but her exclusive boyfriend and Ginger anything but an interloper. Then she thought of Eric. Where did he fit into her life? She enjoyed his company. She respected his knowledge of horses and riding. And she liked the way he had held her hand, liked his easy way of telling her that he had enjoyed the evening and that he had appreciated her invitation.

Thoughts and dreams swirled through her head, intermingling in ways she was hardly aware of, until the telephone jangled around nine o'clock the next morning. Shay heard it, but her sleep-fogged mind didn't come fully to attention until her mother called to her.

"Shay, the phone's for you. Are you awake?"

"I'll get it in the hall, Mom." Shay forced herself from bed long enough to grab the telephone and pull it back into her room. She snuggled under the covers again before she answered, expecting to hear Mollie's voice.

"Hi, Shay," Towe said. "Did I wake you up?"

She came instantly alert. Towe! "Yeah, as a matter of fact I was still asleep, but it's okay. Time I was up and about."

"What did you think of last night?"

Shay was like a fencer, immediately on guard. "I thought it was a good party. How about you?"

"Why don't we go down to the D&D and talk it over, okay?"

"Right now? This morning?"

"You know of a better time?"

Shay stalled. "I thought you had to work."

"Not until this afternoon. I'll pick you up, like in an hour or so, okay?"

"Well, okay, I guess."

"You guess?"

"Well, sure, an hour will be fine. It's just that I have some chores to do."

"So give them the speed treatment, and I'll see you soon."

"Okay, Towe. In an hour."

Shay put the phone back in the hall and hurried to get dressed. She felt as if her feet weren't even touching the floor, she was so happy, so surprised. So her separation from Towe really was just to be a cooling period as he had suggested. They weren't breaking up. Mollie and all the others had been wrong. Towe had called her! He had been out with Ginger last night, but she, Shay Stuart, was the girl he had called this morning.

She did her chores quickly, cleaning her room, making her bed, vacuuming the living room. Then she dressed carefully for the D&D. Green shirt. Green sweater. Jeans. And just enough eye makeup, subtly applied to call attention to her eyes. Towe didn't like lots of makeup on a girl, but he certainly hadn't seemed to mind it on Ginger. She stared at her reflection in the mirror and added a bit more eyeliner. Sometimes, she thought, guys didn't know what they liked until they saw it on another girl. She brushed her bangs, wishing they were longer, much longer.

Towe knocked just as she finished loading linens into the washer. Good. They would be ready for the line or the dryer by the time she got back.

"Hi, Towe." She smiled and opened the door just as she always had done when Towe arrived. "Want to come in for a few minutes before we go?"

"Oh, let's just go on. I could use a soda."

"In the morning?"

Towe glanced at his watch. "It's going toward noon."

"It's ten-thirty. But let's go. I can handle a soda if you can."

Why was Towe making such a big thing of taking her to the D&D on Saturday morning? None of their crowd would be there. Maybe that was his reason. She scowled. Why was she constantly trying to figure Towe out? She used to think she understood him. But that was before Ginger.

Once they were settled in a booth at the D&D with sodas in front of them, Towe came right to the point. "What did you think of last night?"

"It was fine, I suppose."

"You looked as if you were having a good time."

"I said it was fine." She heard the iciness creep into her tone, but she couldn't help it. What did Towe expect her to say, that she couldn't live without him? She wasn't about to say anything that would put Eric down, and so she directed the talk back to Towe. "You seemed to be enjoying yourself, too."

"I was."

"I'm dying to hear all about it."

"Hey, why the sarcasm? We agreed to date others, didn't we? No fair getting all bent out of shape over it."

"I'm not bent out of shape."

"You sound as if you were."

"Well, I'm not." Shay sighed, then looked into Towe's eyes. "Why are we sitting here arguing, Towe? I really didn't like seeing you with Ginger. I didn't like it at all. If you want my honest opinion of last night, I hated it because Ginger was with you and I wasn't."

"I thought you seemed to be hitting it off well with that new guy."

"He's nice enough. But he isn't you. And that makes all the difference in the world."

"I see." Towe poked at the ice cream in his soda with his straw. "It's going to be really hard to make this dating experiment work if you aren't willing to cooperate, Shay."

"I cooperated, didn't I?" Shay finished her soda with a slurp through her straw. "I asked another guy. He accepted the invitation. We appeared together. What more do you want? And how long do you expect this experiment to continue?" She tried to forget that Towe had previously suggested a month or so, hoping he would have forgotten.

"I don't know, Shay. I guess it didn't work out exactly as I had expected it to."

"Just what did you expect?"

"I'm not sure. But I don't like the way I feel about last night, or the way you seem to feel."

"Well, it was your idea. I'm ready to forget it whenever you are." She waited, hoping Towe would agree with her that his idea had been a bummer. But he said nothing and stared at his watch.

"Guess we'd better be going, okay?"

"Suppose so. It's my day to get lunch. Want to stay and take potluck with us?" As soon as the invitation was out she was sorry she had asked. Why did she always seem to say the wrong thing to Towe?

Towe shook his head and glanced at his watch again. "Better get to the garage. Dad's expecting me at noon. Some guy's going to bring his X car in for a diagnosis. It won't go uphill."

"Maybe he should just drive it on level ground." Shay laughed, breaking the tension between them as she slid from the booth. "Thanks for the soda, Towe."

Towe drove her home, leaving immediately, and all the time she was preparing lunch she thought about their strange meeting. Had it been a date? Certainly not a real date. Maybe Towe had just asked her to have a soda with him because he didn't want to take her out that night. Was he going out with Ginger again? The thought tormented her.

That afternoon Shay's mother had more chores for her, and it was late before she arrived at Redhill Ranch to check on Dancer. It didn't surprise her to see Eric's truck in the parking area, but it did surprise her when she saw the worried look on his face when she approached.

"Hi, what's up?" she called out. "Is something the matter?"

"It's Cherokee."

Shay glanced at the horse, which was turning its head and looking balefully at its left side. "What's the trouble?"

"Colic."

Shay looked back at Eric quickly. She had never seen a horse with colic, but she had heard enough about the illness to know that it was serious. "You sure?"

"Positive. Dr. Richards has been here and seen him. He said there's no doubt that Cherokee has colic."

"Is he going to be okay? I mean, if Dr. Richards was here, he wouldn't go off if everything wasn't okay, would he?"

Eric tried to hobble along, bracing himself on one crutch and leading Cherokee with his right hand. "Doc Richards gave him a shot. He said he thought Cherokee had forced the lid from the grain tin and helped himself while nobody was around."

"But how could that have happened? Cherokee was in the pasture and the grain tin was in the feed shed."

"Someone left the pasture gate open. Someone left the lid loose on the grain tin."

"Gosh. That's a tough break." Shay patted Cherokee's withers, but the horse stamped and snorted and kicked at its belly. "I suppose some of those young kids who come out to ride on Saturday mornings were messing around with the grain tins and the gate."

"It doesn't matter who or why at this point, I suppose. It happened. I'm just lucky the vet was handy. But now I have to keep Cherokee walking."

"For how long?" Shay held her breath. She had heard of colicky horses that had had to be walked for hours.

"I have to walk him until he gets to feeling better,

however long that might be. The medicine will help, but the walking is essential.''

"He looks really uncomfortable," Shay admitted as Cherokee stretched his neck back and tried to bite the pain in his belly. "Here, let me walk him around the arena a few times and see what happens." She took the lead rope from Eric, knowing Eric wouldn't last long at leading the horse.

"It's not your problem," Eric said, but he released the lead rope when she pulled on it.

"I'll just spell you for a while." She patted Cherokee on the head. "Come on, boy. Let's take a walk, okay? Come on, boy. Come on, now."

Cherokee followed her, but she had the feeling that if she stopped her own forward motion, she might not get him started again. After three times around the arena, Eric called to her.

"Let me give him a round."

"But you can't."

"I can. And I will. Give me the lead rope."

Shay gave him the rope, wondering how Eric was going to manage. Cherokee looked as if he would lie down and roll at the first chance he got, and she knew he mustn't be allowed to do that. She had heard Dr. Richards say that if a colicky horse once got down, it might be impossible to get him up again. She sat on a stump to rest, and she tried not to watch Eric's painful limping around the ring.

"I've got an idea, Eric," Shay said after Eric had completed one round. "I can tell it's going to take a lot of time to get Cherokee feeling well again. We can't handle this alone."

"I can't call my folks; they've gone away for the weekend. I don't know anyone else to call."

"I do. I'll call Mollie. She'll come out and help us."

"She's probably got a date."

"Maybe not." She felt almost sure that Mollie would be free. "If you can walk him around one more time, I'll make the call from the tack room. Then I'll come back and relieve you, okay?"

"Okay. Tell Mollie I'll pay her."

"She wouldn't accept it as a job, Eric. But as a favor, well, that's a different thing." Shay jogged off before Eric could argue, before Cherokee had a chance to lie down and roll. Grabbing the phone in the tack room, she dialed Mollie.

"Shay, of course I'll come help," Mollie said. "Hang in there." Mollie hung up so quickly Shay had no time to suggest that she bring a sandwich or an apple or something. This was going to be a long night.

Shay ran to where Eric was still struggling to keep Cherokee walking, took the lead rope once more, and urged the horse on around the path. She had never noticed before how red and dusty the arena was, but now the powdery earth smudged against her boots, and it rose in soft puffs from beneath Cherokee's agate-colored hoofs. They were making a fifth turn around the ring when Mollie arrived, driving her family car.

"Ms. McNamara at your service," she called out. "Catering, horse walking, and general spirit raising." She pulled sandwiches from a brown bag, passed one to Eric, another to Shay. "Nothing like a little food to cheer a person up."

"That's what Cherokee thought when he saw the grain

138

tin," Shay said. "But thanks a bunch, Mollie. I'm starving."

"Sandwiches are compliments of your mom, Shay. I called her to give her the news and to warn her that you would probably be late. Didn't figure you had time to call."

"Thanks, Mollie."

"Yeah," Eric said. "I'm starving, too, and I haven't been walking nearly as much as Shay has."

Shay sat down beside Eric near the hitching rail, and they watched Mollie walk Cherokee around the ring a few times. After that they took turns. Shay did five laps. Mollie did five laps. Eric did one lap. And then they started over again. Two hours later the sun fanned red streaks into the sky as it sank below the horizon. Shay watched as the sky turned lavender, gray, then black.

"At least there's going to be a moon," Mollie said as she turned the lead rope over to Shay at nine o'clock. "At least we'll be able to see."

At ten o'clock Shay heard a car approaching. Headlights blinded them for a moment; then Towe called out to them. When he got out of his car he was carrying blankets.

"Towe!" Shay exclaimed, looking at the blankets. "How did you know?"

"Your mom told me the details. She said if you wanted help to call her and she and your father would come out. In the meantime she thought you might need some blankets to wrap up in. It's going to get fairly cool tonight."

"You're a doll, Towe." Mollie grabbed for a blanket.

"And your mom sent a couple of jackets." Towe passed out the jackets; then he ran to the arena where Eric had headed with Cherokee.

"Let me take a turn, man," he called. "Your ankle doesn't need this."

Eric gave up the lead rope and hobbled toward Mollie and Shay, who had wrapped up in the blankets. He and Mollie talked about Cherokee's progress, but Shay was hardly listening to them. Towe had come to help. Towe obviously had called her house. He hadn't had a date with Ginger. He had called her, and he had come out here to help her. Suddenly she didn't care if they had to walk Cherokee all night. What did it matter as long as she was with Towe?

"There are some candy bars in the car," Towe said as Mollie left to take her turn around the ring. "Quick energy. I'll go get them."

"I'm not arguing against it, man," Eric said. "I'm already drooling."

Towe passed out the candy bars, taking one to Mollie before he returned to sit by Shay. "Some Saturday night this is. Never thought I'd be horse sitting."

"Horse walking, you mean," Eric said. "I really appreciate everyone's help."

Eric and Towe talked for a while, and Shay felt as though she would drop from fatigue. This stint reminded her of a time in fourth grade when she decided to stay up all night. To her surprise, nobody had objected, but by midnight she had been so tired that she had fallen asleep in the living-room chair. Now there wasn't even a chair. They had spread one blanket near a tree, and now she just leaned back against the tree trunk and closed her eyes. Dank. She hadn't known Oklahoma nights could be so dank and chilly.

"Hey, Shay," Towe said. "You still with us?"

Shay blinked, rose in a state somewhere between sleep and wakefulness, took her turn at the end of the lead rope. Her feet felt like lead weights, and her eyes felt like sand pits, they burned so badly. But Cherokee was getting better. She felt sure of it. She stopped, and the horse made no attempt to lie down or to kick his belly.

"Poor thing," Shay crooned to him. "You're as tired as we are, aren't you, fellow?" But she kept on walking. She decided to take one more turn around the ring; then she would see what Eric thought about Cherokee. What a night! She was so tired she could hardly move, but deep down inside her she was bubbling with happiness. Towe had chosen to spend the whole night with her, hadn't he? Surely he wouldn't have done that if he didn't really like her. Love her? Maybe their brief "cooling" period had served a good purpose, after all. Maybe one date with Ginger, or maybe seeing her with Eric, had given Towe a new perspective on their relationship. At least he was being civil to Eric. Civil and helpful. That was Towe. She decided there wasn't a jealous bone in his body.

Shay watched the sky slowly change from black to gray to pale bisque. When had a sunrise been so awesome? She laughed at herself. Just how many sunrises had she bothered to look at lately? She walked a bit faster, eager to share the sunrise with Towe, eager to see what Eric thought about Cherokee's condition.

"Hey, I think he's okay," Eric said, watching Cherokee closely for a few moments. "I really think he's over it."

"Looks like it," Towe agreed.

"If it hadn't been for you guys," Eric said, shaking his head. "Listen, there's going to be a pizza celebration on me soon, okay?"

"Okay!" Mollie agreed. "I for one won't let you forget."

"You guys go on now," Eric said. "I'll see you soon. I'd say thanks, but thanks is really a weak word right now. You deserve something much stronger."

"See ya around, Eric." Mollie turned and headed for her car.

Shay started to walk toward her bike, but Towe took her hand. "Leave the bike here, Shay. I'll drive you home and you can come out for it later."

"Okay. I'm too weak to argue." She got into Towe's car, and they rode through the thin, pale dawn in silence. She thought she might go to sleep if someone didn't say something, but she was too tired to start any kind of conversation.

"Shay?"

"What?"

"Shay, I've been doing a lot of thinking these last two days. And, well . . . well, I came out to the ranch tonight to talk with you. But when I saw the bad situation, I just couldn't say what I had planned to say."

"And you want to say it now?" Shay grew cold all over as she guessed what Towe had in mind. But she refused to make it easier for him.

"I think we should break off completely, Shay. We're in a rut. We've closed ourselves off from other people, from fresh ideas. I think we both need a total change of scene.''

Shay didn't trust herself to speak. She opened the car door, slid out quickly, and hurried to her house. She reached the front door, the front hallway, before the sobs rising in her throat choked her and brought her parents on the run.

10

Shay welcomed the comfort of her mother's arms, and after a few moments her sobs subsided and she was able to talk. But she didn't want to talk, at least not about Towe. Not yet. She needed time to herself to think things through and decide just what she was going to do.

"The horse?" her father asked. "It's okay, isn't it?"

"Yes." Shay blew her nose. "Cherokee's going to be all right. He's not in pain any longer."

"You poor thing." Her mother patted her shoulder. "Henry, I told you we should have gone out there to help."

"No, Mom. Towe told us you offered, and we all appreciated it, but there was no sense in you and Dad losing your sleep." She felt tears start to trickle down her cheeks again.

"What you need is a good breakfast and a long, long nap."

"I'm not hungry, Mom. Really, I'm not. Mollie brought the sandwiches you made and Towe had some candy bars." She eased toward her room.

"You're just exhausted," her father said. "If you're really not hungry, why don't you take a hot bath and get right to bed?"

"The bath will relax you," her mother said. "You can sleep all day if you want to."

"Sounds good. I'll go with it." Shay smiled weakly at her parents, then went to her room. Her green room. It certainly suited her now. She was green with envy of Ginger.

A bath! Soaking in hot water might relax her, but it would never make her forget the last few hours, or, more specifically, the last few minutes. She knew Towe's words were permanently etched on her brain. And it was as if her brain had turned into a sound track with no off switch. *I think we should break off completely, Shay. I think we should break off completely, Shay. I think we should break off completely, Shay.*

She held her hands over her ears, but she could still hear his voice, his words. Grabbing her robe and slippers, she hurried into the bathroom. Once she was settled in the tub with frothy bubble bath perfuming the room, Towe's words faded into the background of her thinking. In the foreground was an urgent need to plan a course of action.

What was she going to do? Why had Towe changed his mind so quickly from the idea of dating sometimes to not dating at all? Ginger Netherton. Shay sighed. Ginger was enough to make any guy change his mind about a lot of things. How could she ever compete with Ginger?

Maybe if she hadn't been so sarcastic at the D&D yesterday morning Towe might not have changed his mind. Maybe he could see that dating others as well as each other was going to be a strain and really not any fun at all. Maybe the whole thing had been her fault for not being more broad-minded.

Shay soaked in the warm bath until she caught herself dozing; then she wrapped herself in a thick bath sheet and padded back to her room. How crazy to be putting on pajamas when the sun was just beginning to warm the day. She looked out the window at a squirrel playing under the pecan trees, a blue jay arrowing from the bird feeder to the birdbath. How could everything seem so normal when her world had just come apart like a jigsaw puzzle someone had kicked into the air?

Crawling between the sheets, Shay plumped her pillow and snuggled down to sleep. She had thought that she might never be able to sleep again, that she might lie awake forever thinking about Towe, but that was not the case. She closed her eyes, and the next time she opened them, the sun was slanting through her west window.

She yawned and stretched; then she threw the covers back and rose. She dressed slowly, replaying the night and the early-morning hours in her mind like the rerunning of a horror film.

"You awake, Shay?" her mother called through her door.

"Yes, Mom. I'm up."

"Come on to the kitchen. I've saved some dinner for you."

"I'm not hungry, Mom. Really, I'm not."

"But you have to eat. You'll be sick if you don't eat."

Shay smiled in spite of herself. Her mother seemed absolutely sure that all the sickness in the world was caused by teenagers' refusing to eat the proper food at the proper times. For a moment she stood in front of her mirror smiling at herself. She needed the practice. It wasn't going to be easy to smile from now on. And she had to. She wasn't ready to let her folks know about Towe. Not just yet. She opened the door and walked to the kitchen.

"Towe called you, Shay," her mother said. "He wants you to call him back as soon as you can."

"Okay." She kept her voice very calm, but her throat ached and she couldn't swallow. Towe had called her. Why? To reinforce his decision, just in case she hadn't heard properly?

"You can call him before you eat, if you want to," her mother said.

"No hurry, Mom. I'm hungrier than I thought." Would she spend the rest of her life lying? She thought she would barf if she ate one single bite, but eating was preferable to calling Towe. She wasn't ready for that yet.

"Here's some orange juice and some toast. For heaven's sake, Shay, I don't know if I'm making breakfast or dinner. This mixture will probably make you sick."

"Orange juice and toast are fine, Mom." Shay sipped the orange juice, and it slipped down easier than she had thought it would. But the toast tended to stick in her throat.

"There's some fried chicken left over from our dinner. And some Jell-O salad." Her mother set the food in front of her.

Somehow Shay got through the meal and cleaned up her dishes afterward. But when she went to the telephone, she dialed Mollie, not Towe.

"Hi, Shay," Mollie said through a yawn. "I just this minute got up."

"Me, too, Mol. Just a few minutes ago, that is. Are you busy right now?"

"Haven't decided yet. My day's all turned inside out and backward."

"Yeah, mine too. But I need to talk to you."

"You sound all strung out. Cherokee's okay, isn't he?"

"As far as I know. I haven't talked with Eric this morning—or rather this afternoon."

"Then what's the problem?"

"I need to talk to you in person."

"Want to come over?"

"Why don't we meet at the D&D?"

"Shay! It's Sunday. The D&D's closed."

"Oh, yeah. Right. I forgot. Could you come over here?"

"Sure. If you want me to."

"I want."

"Be there in a few minutes. Got to grab a bite to eat."

"See ya, Mollie. And thanks."

Shay made a pretense of reading the Sunday paper as she waited for Mollie to arrive. When the phone rang, she held her breath and let her mother answer it. What if it was Towe again? She wasn't ready to talk to him. No way.

"Shay, it's for you."

"Is it Towe?"

Her mother shook her head. "It's Eric Chapin."

Shay jumped up and ran to the telephone, surprised at how happy she felt to hear from Eric.

"Hi! How's everything with Cherokee?"

"He's just fine. And am I ever relieved! Don't know how I'm ever going to thank you guys for helping out! But I was serious about us getting together for a pizza. Just the four of us, okay?"

Shay thought fast. She didn't want to hurt Eric's feelings, but neither did she want to set up plans for a cozy pizza foursome that included Towe. "Sounds like fun, Eric. Why don't we talk about it tomorrow at school? We'll see what Mollie has to say."

"Okay. Will do. But I want to thank you again for all the help."

"You're welcome. I have a big interest in Cherokee, too, remember?"

"I'm not about to forget. Will I see you at the ranch tomorrow afternoon?"

"I'm not sure just yet. Sleeping all day has sort of wrecked my study schedule. I may have to hit the books tomorrow."

"Well, see how it goes. If you want a ride to the ranch, I'll be driving out."

"Thanks. And thanks for calling."

After Shay hung up, she was surprised at how pleased she was over Eric's call. She tried to imagine what he would look like if he weren't hunched over a pair of crutches. She wondered idly if he had a girlfriend back in Lawton. He never said much about his past life. Or maybe she just hadn't taken time to ask him about it. When the doorbell rang, she hurried to let Mollie in, and they went straight to her room and closed the door.

"Why so secretive?" Mollie asked, flopping down on the bed, which Shay hadn't even made yet.

149

"Mollie, I'm dying. Simply dying." Shay sat down on the bed, too, feeling the cold brass of the headboard, leaning against it with a pillow to her back. She gulped. "Towe wants us to break up completely." She tried to relax her throat and swallow around the lump that was threatening to block her speech.

"Rats, Shay. I'm really sorry. When did he tell you?"

"This morning when he brought me home. That's why he came out to the ranch in the first place, to talk to me about it. Then, when he saw what a mess we were in out there, he waited."

"What did you tell him?"

"Nothing. I didn't say a word. I just left the car and ran into the house. Mom said he called before I woke up, but I haven't called him back."

"Why not? Maybe he's changed his mind."

"I doubt it. I'm not counting on that. You know how nice he's been to Eric. I think he *wants* Eric to sort of take over, to relieve him. He's never acted jealous of Eric, and that really tells me something."

"Yeah, it does, at that."

"I just wish I knew how to handle this. You know what I mean, Mollie. I don't know what to do or what to say. I don't want to look like a complete nerd."

"Yeah. It's really tough to break up, isn't it? I knew it would be. I've never gone steady, but I just know how tough it would be to break up."

"You can't really *know*, Mollie. But you're so good at coming up with answers. I thought maybe you could help."

"You don't want to break up?"

"Of course not. I mean, Towe's *everything* to me."

150

"But you don't want to go out with a guy who doesn't want to go out with you, do you?"

Shay thought for a moment as Mollie put the situation into a different perspective. "No, of course I don't want that. I guess what I want is for Towe to want to go out with me. I wish things were just as they used to be."

"Life goes on, Shay. That's a cliché. But it's true. You've got to adjust. Maybe you should call Towe and really talk over your feelings with him."

"Not yet." Shay looked at Mollie without smiling. "Mollie, pretend it's ten years from now. Pretend you're a famous psychologist and I'm a patient coming to you for help. What would you say?"

"Rats, Shay. You're really putting me on the spot. It's not ten years from now. I'm not any kind of a psychologist. I don't want to be responsible for maybe messing up your life."

"Then you're not going to help me?"

"I didn't say that."

"Mol! Come on. Either you're going to try to help or you're not going to try to help. Which is it going to be?"

"Maybe you should just sort of try to think things through for yourself, Shay. When you get right down to it, psychology is just a matter of using a lot of common sense."

"It is?"

"Sure. When a person's in a bad spot, she has to stop and consider what action she can take. That's using common sense, isn't it?"

"I'd like to crawl in a hole and hide. I wish school were out so I wouldn't have to face any of the kids again, especially not Towe Williams or Ginger Netherton."

"Hiding in a hole is hardly one of your choices. You've got to be practical about this. You do have some choices, you know. You're not the first girl in the world who's been jilted by her steady."

Shay winced at Mollie's use of the word *jilted*, unable to reply.

"But you've got a lot going for you. There's Eric, for instance. It's not so bad to lose one guy when you've got another guy waiting in the wings."

"Eric's not waiting in the wings. We're just friends because we both like riding, because circumstances have thrown us together."

"Okay. Okay. Back to Towe. You have some choices of action besides hiding. For instance, you could make a big scene at school. You could cry and carry on and make him feel like a real heel. If there's anything a guy hates, it's a public crying scene. He might come back to you just to hush you up."

Shay scowled and sat up straighter. "I'm not about to make a scene. No way. It would just make me look really gross and really rejected."

"I agree. Making a big scene can be a messy thing. My mom calls it washing your dirty linen in public. So let's forget crying jags. If you want to be really dramatic, you could call Towe as he asked you to do, and threaten suicide. That should get his full attention."

"Suicide!" Shay shook her head. "What about common sense, Mollie? I'm not about to threaten suicide."

"I didn't think you'd go for that idea, either of those ideas. So you've got to come up with something else."

"Maybe I should just act as if I don't care. I could come on as if nothing important had happened."

"Everyone would know you were faking."

152

"Yeah. Everyone would know. There's just no easy solution, is there?"

"There's my solution." Mollie grinned at her. "Don't get so involved in the first place. But, of course, it's a little too late for that, isn't it?"

"I don't think it's a very good solution anyway, Mollie. A person can't go around avoiding involvement because she might get hurt."

"So what are you thinking?"

"Maybe a person should imagine scales, imagine all the good feelings involved in a relationship on one side of the scale and all the bad feelings on the other side."

"And you think the good feelings will overbalance the bad ones?"

"Yeah, I really do, Mol. I feel lousy right now, but Towe and I have had some super times together. Mol, I'm glad you came over. You helped me understand that."

"But I didn't help you understand anything. I just, well . . . Shay, you've reached some sort of a decision, haven't you? I can tell. Give. What is it? What are you going to say to Towe?"

"I'm still not sure. Not really. I feel rotten about breaking up with him, but you're right. I don't want to go with a guy who doesn't want to go with me. I'm just going to take it one day at a time, Mollie. And I'm going to hang on to my self-respect."

"Good thinking." Mollie rose and walked toward the door. "If you're not doing anything this coming weekend, I may get up a slumber party. Sue and Beth, you know. The four of us. We haven't done that in a long time. What do you think?"

"It really sounds good, Mollie. It really does." She

walked to the door with Mollie. "Thanks a bunch for coming over. Just talking with you helps me sort out things in my own mind."

Shay watched as Mollie backed her car from the driveway; then she turned toward the telephone. In the privacy of her room she dialed Towe's number, and when he answered she got right to the point.

"Mom said you called, Towe, and I wondered if we could get together sometime tomorrow to talk for a few minutes."

"Why, sure, Shay. That's just what I wanted to ask you, if we couldn't get together and talk things over. I mean, you know, like the D&D after school?"

"No. I think we need more privacy than that. If you have your car, why don't we just drive somewhere where we can be alone for a few minutes?"

"Fine. I'll see you at your locker after school."

"Thanks, Towe." Shay hung up quietly and stared into space for a few minutes. She had made it over the first hurdle. She had talked with Towe without crying. In fact, there had been no threat of tears. Maybe she should go out for drama club. These next days were going to require a lot of acting ability, but she was determined that this breakup was going to be handled with dignity on her part. No matter how sad and bereft and dejected she felt, she was going to put on a class act.

On Monday morning Shay dressed very carefully in gold slacks and a pale gold sweater. She trimmed her bangs with a razor blade, making them look wispier than ever. That was the way she felt today, wispy. Mollie was waiting for her on the corner nearest her house, and if Shay had been in a better mood, she would have smiled at the contrast between them. Mollie was wearing jeans with a bright red shirt, a red headband around her blunt-cut hair.

"Hi, Mollie!" Shay called. Then, when she reached Mollie's side, she lowered her voice. "Really glad you waited for me."

"Thought you might be," Mollie said. "Did you call Towe yesterday evening?"

"Yeah. We're going to have a talk after school. I'm not looking forward to it, but on the other hand, I've sort of prepared myself for it. I know exactly what I'm going to say."

"Want to rehearse your lines?"

"No, thanks. I'll manage okay, Mol. But what a bummer. I feel rotten."

"Yeah. I can imagine."

As they approached the school grounds Eric came toward them, swinging along on his crutches as if they hardly bothered him at all.

"Hi," Mollie called out. "Cherokee still okay?"

"He's fine. I went to the stable early this morning. He looked great."

"I'm glad. With that big show coming up next Saturday, we'll really have to get busy training."

"But not today," Eric said. "Doc Richards said to rest him a couple of days. Maybe you can work him about Wednesday."

"Good deal. I'll be ready."

"Since we can't ride today, how about that pizza I promised you? I talked to Towe, but he begged off. He says he's on some kind of diet. But the rest of us can go, can't we?"

"Sounds good to me," Mollie said. "I could eat pizza three times a day."

"Yeah, me, too," Shay agreed.

"I'll pick you both up tonight around six o'clock, okay? You don't mind riding in a truck, do you?"

"Wheels are wheels," Mollie said. "Who's being picky?"

"See you then." Eric smiled and swung off toward the schoolhouse door.

Shay wasn't surprised that Towe had bagged out on the pizza dinner, nor was she surprised to realize that she was relieved. Eric's pizza treat would be more fun for everyone this way.

Somehow the school day passed. Morning classes were the slowest. And the lunch hour really dragged, in spite of Mollie's inviting her to eat with her and Chip. All three of them pretended not to see Towe sitting with Ginger and the senior crowd.

After school Towe met Shay at her locker. She could feel the glances of the kids passing by. It was as if they were silently asking just who Towe Williams was going with, Shay or Ginger. And she could feel them all betting on Ginger.

"Ready?" Towe smiled, but he didn't offer to carry her books as he usually did.

"Yes. Let's go."

They walked from the building and got into his car. Shay held her books in front of her like a shield, and she said nothing until Towe drove to a little-used road near Redhill Ranch and parked the car. He cleared his throat; Shay waited for him to speak first.

"Shay, I'm sorry if I've hurt you. I've tried not to, you know."

"I'll live, Towe. Don't worry about it."

"I wanted to talk to you Saturday night, but then there

was the horse problem. It was really no time for talking.''

''Right.'' What had happened to all the words she had planned? Where had they disappeared to?

''Is that all you're going to say?''

''What did you expect me to say?'' Could he tell she was stalling, or did he think she was being aloof? Mysterious?

''I don't know. I guess I really don't know what I did expect. But you could make this talk a little easier for me.''

''Why should I do that?'' Why, indeed!

''Because we're still going to be friends, aren't we?''

''I hope so, Towe. And you're right. I wasn't being fair. Friends should make things easier for each other. I'm sorry we're breaking up.''

''Yeah, I am, too.''

For a moment Shay waited, hoping Towe would say he had changed his mind, that it all had been a big mistake on his part. But he didn't. Obviously, he wasn't that sorry about the split.

''Shay, there comes a time when a relationship should end. I've felt it coming for several weeks, and I think, if you're honest with yourself, you'll admit you felt it coming, too.''

''No. I didn't, Towe. And I *am* being honest with myself. With both of us. I wanted things to go on just as they had been.''

''You won't have any trouble finding another boy-friend. You know that, don't you?''

Shay shrugged, corking words that would reveal her breaking heart.

''I mean, you and Eric seem to hit it off very well.''

She held her voice very steady. "Eric and I do have a lot in common, I suppose, but . . ."

"Shay, if you'll be really honest with yourself, you'll admit that about all we were getting from our relationship was comfort."

"Comfort?"

"Yes. The comfort of knowing we had a date for the next event, whatever it might be. And for this feeling of comfort we were cutting ourselves off from a lot of things. Other friends. Hobbies. Or maybe we were just cutting ourselves off from free time for thinking, for being alone with our thoughts."

"I suppose you're right, Towe." Shay took a deep breath and then began saying all the things she had planned to say, forcing so much sincerity into her voice that she almost believed her words. If she hadn't been crying deep down inside herself in that private spot where only she lived, she would have believed herself, she sounded so logical.

"I won't be able to forget you quickly, Towe. Surely you know that. But you're right. We have grown apart. It was just so nice being your special girl that I hated to give it up. I'll always remember your voice." She paused a moment for effect. "Did you know I sometimes thought of you as the boy with the Pied Piper voice?"

Towe smiled. "Really?"

"Yeah, really. And your smile, Towe. I'll always remember your smile, the way it lights up your whole face. It's been nice being known as Towe Williams's girl, and I want you to know I'll always be your friend. Okay?"

"Okay." Towe smiled at her and reached for her

hand, but she avoided his touch. Opening the car door, she stepped out and closed it behind her.

"Hey," Towe called. "What's the deal?"

"You go on, Towe. No big deal. I just want to be alone for a few minutes. I'll walk home. It's not all that far. And the walk will give me some thinking time." She paused a moment before she turned to leave. Then she looked back and called over her shoulder, "See ya around, Towe."

11

To Shay's surprise, she didn't cry as she walked away from Towe. The parting had been that easy. And that hard. She had made it over a second big hurdle, meeting Towe face to face. She even smiled to herself a bit. She knew from the look in Towe's eyes that he had felt just a little unsure of himself. She hoped he was wondering if perhaps he hadn't made a mistake. She had intended for him to wonder. She held herself very straight and tall as she walked toward home.

At six o'clock Eric knocked on the door. His broad grin almost distracted her from noticing that he was no longer on crutches.

"Eric! You're walking!"

"Right. Got rid of the sticks this afternoon. Doc says I can walk, as long as I take it easy."

"What about riding?" Shay tried not to hold her breath as she waited for his answer. If he could ride, then she was again without a mount for the first show.

"No riding for another two weeks. Doc said it was one of the worst sprains he has ever seen—almost worse than a broken bone. I'm strictly grounded as far as Cherokee is concerned.''

"I'd be lying if I said I was disappointed." Shay shook her head. "But I know how much you want to ride. I know it's really tough on you."

"I'll survive. It helps to know Cherokee's in good hands."

Now Shay noticed that Mollie was already in the truck. Eric had picked Mollie up first. But what did that matter? In fact, maybe it was for the best. She didn't want to rebound to any boy just yet, and it would be very easy to rebound right to Eric if he gave her half a chance.

She climbed into the truck beside Mollie, and Eric drove them to Utica Square in the inner city. A stucco house with a red tile roof had been converted into a pizza palace, but Shay forgot the ordinary look of the place as she inhaled the mingled fragrances of oregano, bacon, anchovies.

"What'll you have?" Eric asked after they sat down at a booth near the jukebox. "Sky's the limit, or ten dollars, whichever comes first."

"Why don't we share a large size?" Mollie asked. "Okay?"

"A large with everything on it?" Eric asked. "And a pitcher of Coke."

"Sounds good to me," Shay agreed.

After the waitress took their order, they talked about school, about the upcoming horse show, about everything but the person most on Shay's mind. Towe. Nobody mentioned his name. And because everybody so carefully avoided his name, she knew Eric and Mollie were thinking of him, too.

When the waitress brought their order, the pizza was still steaming. The fragrance made Shay's mouth water until she almost drooled. If she had truly been in love with Towe, surely she couldn't have eaten a bite. Her appetite would have been gone. Maybe she was going to recover from Towe more quickly than she had thought. Maybe eating pizza was the first step to take toward mending a broken heart. She took a bite. Then suddenly her appetite left her. Pizza was not the remedy.

"Hey, eat up," Eric said.

"Burned my tongue," Shay lied.

"Yeah, I always do that right on the first bite." Mollie spooned ice from her glass. "Suck on this. Ice helps."

Shay held the ice on her tongue for a few minutes to hide her vanished appetite. Then she managed to eat a small wedge of the pizza and start on another wedge. Eric had appetite enough to make up for her own lack. He managed to finish everything she and Mollie couldn't eat, leaving only a few crumbs on the tin.

"It was great, Eric," Mollie said. "Be sure to call me first if you need any more horse walking. Fair trade."

"Yeah," Shay agreed. "Neat treat, Eric."

Eric drove Shay home first, and it was almost an hour before Mollie called her.

"Hey, Eric's really a neat guy, Shay. He's really interesting to talk to."

"Yeah. He knows a lot more about horses and horse training than a lot of the experts."

"He knows a lot about a lot of things."

"Hey, you really like him? I mean, maybe you two could be an item." Shay tried to sound enthusiastic, but it wasn't as easy as she had thought it would be.

"Not so fast, Shay. This is me, Mollie, you're talking to. I'm not hunting for that tie that binds. Eric's an okay guy, but so is Chip. So are a lot of guys who never give me the time of day."

"Okay. Okay. No lectures, please." Shay sighed, glad that Mollie wasn't wanting to latch on to Eric as a steady partner.

"Did you and Towe have that talk?" Mollie asked. "Or is that question off limits?"

"Not off limits. We talked. No tears. No threats. A class act from beginning to end."

"Good deal, Shay. I'm glad you didn't pitch a fit. You'll never regret it."

"I suppose not." What else was there to say?

"It'll hurt for a while, but you'll mend."

"You busy, Mollie?"

"Right now?"

"Yeah, right now."

"What do you have in mind?"

"Going shopping. The stores at the mall are open on Monday night, you know. I feel like going on a binge. A clothes-buying binge. I'd like to appear at school tomorrow as the new me."

"And what's the new you going to look like?"

"I don't know yet. Why don't I pick you up in about five minutes, and we'll go to the shops and decide what the new me is going to look like."

"You're high on freedom, Shay. I never ride with anyone who's high. *I'll* pick *you* up, okay?"

"Deal."

Shay emptied her piggy bank, and then she emptied a small cache of bills and coins from a box in the back of her underwear drawer. Only fifteen dollars. She couldn't go on much of a binge with no more than that. But when Mollie arrived, she ran to her car.

"I want a new haircut, a new T-shirt, maybe some new makeup," Shay announced as she got in the car.

"What'd you do, rob a bank?"

"Yeah, my own. Found fifteen dollars."

"A new hairstyle will take most of that," Mollie said.

"Maybe I'll start with the T-shirt. I could always cut my hair myself."

"Sure you could! But you wouldn't, would you? I mean, if you mess it up, it'll take ages for it to grow out."

"I'd like a pixie cut. You know, sort of a chopped-off look with very short, wispy bangs."

"You'll need an appointment. You can't just walk into a salon and expect instant service. Shay?"

"What?"

"I could do the cut for you. I mean, if you'd trust me to do it. I do my mom's all the time, and she looks pretty good."

"Deal! Mollie, this is exciting! The new me. I'm really sick of this long hair. I've just kept it long because Towe liked it so much. Now, with summer coming and the show season opening, it'll be a lot more practical to have short hair."

Shay's excitement mounted when they reached the mall and she found just the right T-shirt at the Shirt Shop.

"You sure you want orange?" Mollie asked. "It's really bright."

"My new color. I'm tired of being a pastel mouse."

"Mice aren't pastel. You've flipped."

"And I want orange sneakers to match the shirt. I'll bag the makeup in favor of sneakers."

"I don't think anyone makes orange sneakers," Mollie said. But she was wrong. They found a pair at Kresge's.

"For only five ninety-five, at least they won't last forever," Mollie said, giggling. "Why are you doing this to yourself, Shay? Everyone's going to notice you tomorrow. Are you sure that's what you want?"

"They'll be noticing the *new* Shay Stuart, and that's fine. Mollie, the old Shay is gone forever."

"I don't know if that's good or bad. I'll have to read up in some psych books and see if I can find out."

"Don't tell me what you learn unless it's good," Shay said.

After they finished shopping, they went to Shay's house and Mollie got ready to cut her hair. Comb. Razor blade. Towel.

"Don't you want to watch?" Mollie asked. "Get a mirror."

"Better I should not watch. I might change my mind. And I don't want to change my mind."

Mollie cut Shay's hair, using a razor, wetting the hair down as she needed to, and when she finished she smiled. "Not bad, if I do say so myself, Shay. Not half bad. You look like a dandelion."

"Good grief!" Shay shrieked and ran to the bathroom mirror. "Hey! I like it! But it's a little long on the left side just behind the ear."

Mollie looked carefully and nodded. "Yeah, you're right." She nipped off another bit of hair and waited while Shay took a second look.

"And how about right here on the crown?" Shay lifted a long piece of hair. "Just a little shorter, huh?"

Again Mollie nipped off the strand. "That's it, Shay. No more. Live with it this way a day or so; then, if you want more cut off, we'll see about it, okay?"

"Okay, Mol!" She grinned at her. "You're the best friend a girl ever had."

"Thanks a bunch. Your folks will probably be after my scalp tomorrow. Don't tell them who did it to you, okay?"

"Okay, but it looks fine. Looks just the way I want to look. Think I'll call it the happy-dandelion look."

Shay walked out to the car with Mollie, and when she returned to the house she showed her new hairdo and her shirt and shoes to her parents.

"What brought all this on?" her mother asked.

"It's the new me."

"I liked the old you," her father said. "Of course, I like the new you, too. But orange shoes? I'll never in this world understand women!"

Shay told her parents good night, but once she reached her room she knew that new clothes and a new haircut weren't going to make up for losing Towe. They were just stage props in the act she was putting on.

On Tuesday morning Mollie again stopped by for Shay, and with Mollie at her side Shay felt a rush of confidence. Of course, she felt self-conscious about her new haircut, her new shirt and shoes, but at least those feelings took her mind off Towe.

"You look great," Mollie said. "You'll have everyone turning for a second glance."

"That's not exactly what I had in mind," Shay said.

"I just need to feel as if I'm starting out on a new adventure. Alone."

"No gal's alone as long as she's wearing orange shoes." Mollie giggled. "Listen, Shay, I called Beth and Sue last night after I got home. They're going to meet us in the lunchroom today."

"Thanks, Mollie. But I don't want you to feel that you have to give up eating with Chip. No way."

"I'm not tied to Chip, Shay. I eat with whomever I want to. And today I'm lunching with my three best friends."

The bell rang just as they reached the school grounds, and Mollie and Shay parted. To Shay's surprise, Eric was waiting at her locker.

"Like wow!" he exclaimed. "You've done something to your hair."

"It's a new invention called cutting." Shay grinned, glad that Eric had noticed. "Thought a short cut would be better for the show ring this summer."

"Right. Judges go for the neat, trim look. Long hair can get in the way if a rider isn't careful."

Shay unlocked her locker and began pulling out books for her morning classes. Was Eric going to escort her down the hall? Why was he hanging around? Not that she minded. Not that she minded at all.

"I just stopped by to see if you want to go to the ranch right after school. Dad's still letting me use the truck, so if you want a ride, you're welcome."

"Deal," Shay said. "I need to work Cherokee in the ring every afternoon this week, Eric. We just won't be ready for that show if I don't."

"I know. But this afternoon's session's going to have

167

to be a short one, okay? Don't want to overtire him. You can ease into a full workout by Thursday, I think.''

"Okay. See you after school." She had said it casually, with no self-consciousness. She had never felt that easy around Towe. She had always waited for him to speak out, always wondered if she had said the right thing at the right time. But Eric was different. He wasn't her boyfriend. He was just a friend who happened to be a boy. There was a lot of difference.

Shay was glad the morning seemed to pass quickly. She had been afraid it would drag by with her thinking more about Towe than about her lessons. She hadn't even seen Towe. And maybe it was for the best. But she was going to have to get used to seeing him, seeing him and realizing he no longer was hers. How silly that she had ever thought of him in such a way. A person couldn't own another person. That was a comforting thought. If she couldn't own Towe, neither could Ginger. Comforting. She almost hated the word. That's how Towe had described their relationship. A matter of comfort. How could she have been so dumb as to have mistaken comfort for love?

"Stop thinking about Towe," Mollie said as they met and walked to the lunchroom.

"So now you're a mind reader?"

"When you get that sad, dejected look, it isn't hard to figure out who you're thinking about. Come on! I think we're having goulash today."

"Big deal." Shay sighed, but she smiled as Beth and Sue joined them.

"Hey, gang," Sue said, easing her pudgy body into the lunch line, "let's fill our trays and take them out under the maples to eat. It's okay as long as we bring everything back inside when we're through."

"Okay with me," Mollie said. "Beth?"

"Sure, I'm game. It'll be like a picnic, and we could do with a little privacy today."

Had Beth emphasized the word *today?* Shay studied Beth in her black slacks, black shirt. The outfit made her look tall and thin, and her Dutch-bobbed hair and blue eyes seemed rather out of place. Or maybe it was all the black that was out of place. Beth was never somber.

Goulash. Tossed salad. Crackers. Milk. The lunch line moved quickly, and once they were settled under the maples, Shay was glad they had decided to eat outside. There was a pleasant light breeze, and she watched the sunlight make gray lacy patterns on the grass as it filtered through the leaves.

"Give, Shay." Sue turned her face to the sun in a way that accented her freckles. "We want to hear all about it."

"All about what?" Suddenly Shay knew she couldn't eat a bite. Nor did she intend to answer questions. She was counting on silence to add to her mystique. How could Sue make such a direct approach? That was more Mollie's style.

"What did Towe *say?*" Sue asked. "And what did *you* say? I hope you really told him off. He's got a nerve dropping you for Ginger Netherton."

"Who said Towe dropped Shay?" Mollie asked. "I heard it was just the other way around."

Good old Mollie. Shay smiled at her.

"Give, Shay," Beth said. "What really happened between you and Towe?"

"Nothing really happened." Shay shrugged in what she hoped was a nonchalant way. But she fought a desire to reveal all, to tell them how she really felt. She could certainly use a little sympathy, and she knew it would be forthcoming from these friends. She hadn't even told her parents about the breakup yet. Mollie was the only one who really knew how bad she felt. No. That wasn't right. Even Mollie didn't know all. Nobody could really know or really understand her feelings except her.

"Well, something must have happened," Beth said. "One day you're going steady with Towe, and the next day he's eyeing Ginger and you're eyeing Eric Chapin."

"Eric and I are just friends." Shay took a bite of goulash. "We just happen to keep our horses at the same ranch."

"And you just happened to invite him to the mixer," Sue said. "And he just happened to take you out for pizza."

"Say," Beth said, leaning closer to Shay. "There's a rumor going around school that you and Eric . . . well, that you and Eric spent the night together. The whole night, on a moonlight horseback ride."

Mollie giggled. "Shay, you'd better speak up. The rumors are getting out of hand."

"Look, guys," Shay said. "No big deal, see?" And she told them all about Cherokee and the colic and everyone's part in the all-night vigil.

"The all-night walk had nothing to do with Eric and me, guys. Really, it didn't. Towe was right there all the time. We just decided by mutual agreement that we needed more space in our relationship." How could she be saying that? How could she be so calm when she felt as if she were coming apart inside?

"So we're going to date others, maybe for a while, maybe permanently. We'll just take it day by day and see how it goes. Towe and I have a lot of respect for each other."

Lunch period ended, and Shay knew she had made it over a third hurdle, facing the girls and their questions. She felt proud of herself for keeping her private feelings really private. And she hoped Towe would do the same. They really did have a lot of respect for each other.

After school she and Eric drove to the ranch and worked Cherokee as they had planned. Then Eric helped her groom Dancer. After they were finished, they got back into the truck, and Eric drove slowly along a sunny country road.

"Where are you going?" Shay asked.

"No place special. It's just so nice to be outside. At least I can ride the truck, even if I can't ride Cherokee."

"Eric! Look!"

"Where?"

Shay pointed to a thicket laced with white frothy blossoms. "Over there. It's wild blackberries again."

"Again?" Eric stopped the truck beside the blackberry growth.

Shay felt herself flush. She didn't want to repeat Towe's tale about Blackberry Winter. She thought fast. "I mean, I saw wild blackberries in bloom about two weeks ago. I guess I just didn't realize they bloomed for so long a time."

"They don't, Shay. It's just that each clump is individual. Blackberry plants are clones. Each plant reproduces plants exactly like itself. Some bloom early; some bloom late. Guess these are late bloomers."

"They're so beautiful." She gazed at the blossoms

that cascaded in white masses against a green backdrop of leaves.

"I'll pick you a bouquet." Eric opened the truck door and stepped to the ground.

"Oh, but they have thorns," Shay said. "You'll get scratched."

"Who's afraid of a few thorns?" Eric laughed. "If you like blackberry blossoms, I'll give you blackberry blossoms." He pulled a pocketknife from his jeans, strode to the bushes, and cut off five sprigs, shaving off the thorns before he returned to the truck and handed them to Shay.

"Eric, thanks!" She buried her nose in the fragrant blossoms. "I'll take them home and put them in water." She had been looking at the flowers, and when she glanced up at Eric, he was smiling at her. His eyes were such a deep green they were like dark mirrors reflecting the image of the blackberry blossoms.

They rode home without speaking and with the fragrance of blackberry blossoms filling the space and the pleasant silence between them.

Shay told Eric goodbye, and she slipped from the truck before he could open the door for her. She hurried into the house and put the blackberry blossoms in a vase, which she set on the drop-leaf table in the kitchen.

"Oh, how pretty," her mother said when she came in. "Where did you find them?"

"Out by the ranch. Eric picked them for me and trimmed away the thorns."

Shay set the table, and then she said what she had been dreading to say. "Mom, Towe and I have broken up."

172

"I guessed something was wrong between you," her mother said. "But I didn't want to pry."

"And I didn't want to tell you until I could tell you without crying. It was his idea, Mom, not mine."

"That makes it harder to take, doesn't it?"

"Yeah. Lots harder. Mom, did you ever lose a guy that you really liked?" Shay was surprised at her own question. She could hardly imagine her mother as a young girl with boyfriends.

"Yes, Shay. I doubt that there's a girl in the world who hasn't lost the guy she thought she absolutely couldn't live without. I lost a few, but I survived."

"Do you ever think about them—think about them and wish it might have turned out differently?"

"No."

"Honest?"

"Honest."

Shay was surprised when her mother suddenly broke into laughter. "Mom! What's so funny?"

"I really hadn't thought of those old boyfriends in a long time, Shay. Your question took me back over a lot of years. One boy married a classmate of mine, and they had ten children the last time I heard. I like kids, but I wouldn't want to change places with that lady. And another old beau has been married and divorced four times. That's not for me, either. Sometimes fate protects us, Shay. I know you think you'll never forget Towe, and you probably won't. You wouldn't really want to forget him altogether. It'll help you through this time if you try to remember and to believe that all things happen for the best."

"Do you really believe that, Mom?"

"Sometimes. Most times. Anyway, I try to live as if I believed it." Her mother smiled at her. "Call your dad now. Let's have supper."

Supper had been over for quite a while, but it was still light outside when someone knocked on the door. Shay went to answer.

"Mollie! Come on in."

"No. How about you coming out? Look who's with me."

Shay glanced at Mollie's car, and Randy waved to her from the window.

"Sorry we didn't call ahead, Shay, but Randy wonders if we can go to the stable so he can take a picture of Dancer."

"Whatever for?"

"Come on out to the car and he can tell you what he has in mind."

Shay told her parents she was leaving, then hurried to the car with Mollie. Randy got out, motioned her into the middle of the front seat, and climbed in after her.

"Glad you were home, Shay. I hitched a ride to Tulsa with some buddies. Would have called ahead had I known they were coming this way."

"It's okay. Mollie says you want a picture of Dancer. What's the deal?"

"It's just an idea, but it might work into a term paper or even a magazine article sometime. I'm going to start a photo collection of unusual animals and write a short piece to go along with each photo. There are a lot of unusual things that go on in the animal world, and a mare expecting twin foals is one of them. Do you mind if I take a pic?"

"Of course not." Shay glanced at the sky. "Is there still enough light?"

"Doesn't matter. I've got a flash attachment."

They drove to the ranch, and Shay whistled for Dancer. The mare took her time walking to the fence, and Shay gave her extra pats and attention once she reached them.

"Want Shay in the picture?" Mollie asked. "Horse and owner?"

"No," Randy said. "Just horse."

Shay stood behind Randy, snapping her fingers so Dancer would prick her ears forward and look alert. Just as they finished the picture taking, Eric arrived in his truck.

"What's going on?" he called as he joined them. Then he hesitated as he saw Randy and realized he didn't know him.

"My cousin, Randy Russell," Mollie said, explaining the picture-taking session.

"What's the matter, Eric?" Shay asked. "What are you doing back out here?"

"Just came to make one more check on Cherokee. Guess I've just got the jitters since that bout of colic."

"He's fine," Shay said. "See, there he is down by the creek."

Eric whistled, and Cherokee cantered toward them. When Eric was sure the gelding was okay, he turned to get into his truck again. Then he paused.

"How about a soda at the D&D?" he asked, looking directly at Mollie.

Mollie turned to Randy. "How about it, Randy? Got the time?"

"Sure. Just so I'm out at Tulsa U. to meet my buddies in about an hour."

"How about riding with me, Mollie?" Eric asked. "Can Randy handle the car?"

"Sure," Randy answered for Mollie. "You go ahead. Shay and I'll be right behind you."

Shay laughed and got into Mollie's car beside Randy. What a day it had been! Riding with Eric. Going for a soda with Randy. And all of it so unplanned. Suddenly she was enjoying a new sense of freedom, a sense of being able to cope with boys. But would the feeling last? She had spent almost a whole school year taking her identity from Towe. Could she cope on her own?

"What are you thinking about that makes you frown so?" Randy asked.

Shay smiled immediately. "I didn't realize I was frowning. I should be smiling, shouldn't I? It's not every day that Shay Stuart gets to go to the D&D with a college man."

"As I said once before, flattery will get you everywhere." Randy grinned at her. "Why, I might even treat you to a banana split with nuts, chocolate, and a cherry on top."

Shay giggled, not even caring that Randy Russell was probably much too sophisticated to pay much attention to a giggly high-school girl. It had been Dancer's picture he wanted, hadn't it? Not hers.

And why did she feel like giggling? Mollie had just driven off with Shay's favorite riding partner, yet she was laughing. Towe had dropped out of her life at his request. Mollie was with Eric. And she knew she couldn't depend on Randy for any dates. Oklahoma U.

was a long way from Tulsa. Yet she was laughing, and it felt good. Maybe, just maybe, she didn't need to depend on any one boy for dates or anything else. Maybe she was learning to be Shay Stuart, a girl with orange shoes and hair like a dandelion who could manage her own life.

12

The next days passed quickly with teachers pouring on end-of-the-year homework, but Shay managed to get it all done and still have time each day to spend an hour or so at the ranch working Cherokee, preparing him for the Saturday-afternoon show.

"What are you going to wear?" Mollie asked Shay on Saturday after they had eaten early lunch together in Shay's kitchen.

Shay looked at her watch. "Come on. I'll show you." She led the way down the hallway to her bedroom. "It's nothing new, but it's my favorite riding outfit." She laid out black riding pants and chaps, tan turtleneck shirt, black-and-tan tailored jacket.

"Neat!" Mollie picked up a black riding boot and polished its toe on her jeans. "Better get into all this stuff. It's almost time to get out to the arena."

Shay grabbed a pair of white gloves and her black riding hat and tossed them onto the bed. Then she began dressing. When she had finished, she looked around carefully to make sure she hadn't forgotten anything.

"I won't put the chaps on until the last minute.

They're really long and heavy. Let's do it, Mollie. I'm about to go bananas just worrying about everything."

"It doesn't show. You look calm enough."

"Good luck, Shay," her mother called as Shay said goodbye. "Your father and I will be out later in time to see you ride."

"I'll look for you."

Thank goodness Mollie was driving. Shay was so nervous that it felt good to relax for a few minutes. She knew she had to calm down or Cherokee would sense her mood and get nervous, too. She wanted him to be fully collected but not overly excited. There was a fine line between the two conditions; Cherokee and Eric were depending on her to find it.

"You're really quiet," Mollie said. "Scared?"

"No. Just thinking. I'm glad this first show's at the Redhill arena. Cherokee's used to working out there. And it's always an advantage not to have to trailer a horse to the show ring."

"Is Eric meeting you at the stable?"

Shay nodded and pulled her hat lower onto the back of her head. "He went out early to groom Cherokee. He'll have him all saddled and ready for me. I really feel sorry for him, Mol."

"Who? Eric or Cherokee?"

"Eric. I know how much he'd like to be riding in this show."

"Well, he's lucky his horse is in the show. Look at it that way. You're doing him a big favor."

When they reached the ranch, Mollie parked the car in a pasture near the main road. Shay felt the tingle of excitement she always felt when she arrived at the show arena on show day. Crowds of riders and spectators

179

milled around the show ring and around a temporary refreshment stand which the Junior Saddle Club members always ran to raise money for the group. Country-western music blared from a black loudspeaker which had been rigged up at the far end of the refreshment stand. The pasture used for parking was beginning to fill up with cars and trucks which were pulling single- and double-stall horse trailers.

"I see the Whortons are here." Shay nodded to a green school bus towing a four-stall trailer.

"Bet your folks are glad they didn't have two sets of twins who all liked to ride," Mollie said. "Pulling four horses around the country must be a real scene."

"Yeah." Shay headed for the stable. "But they say that at every show at least one of the Whorton kids usually goes home with a trophy."

Shay left Mollie and hurried on to Cherokee's stall, inhaling the mingled odors of horseflesh, saddle leather, straw. When she saw Eric and Cherokee, she grinned.

"Neat, Eric. Very neat. I've never seen Cherokee look so good." She patted the Appaloosa's head, then ran her hand along his gleaming withers.

"I gave him a bath this morning, and I just finished polishing his hoofs." Eric stood back to admire his work. "He does look good, doesn't he?"

"Think I'll give him a practice turn around the ring," Shay said. "Okay?"

"Good idea."

She mounted and rode to the arena gate. She was about to enter the ring when she saw Towe and Ginger. The sudden tears that burned behind her eyelids surprised her. She had thought she was over that reaction. Towe was wearing a forest-green shirt and his best jeans, and Ginger was in a similar outfit. Had she bought a new wardrobe just to match up with Towe's? Shay blinked away her tears and made herself concentrate on Cherokee as she put him through his paces.

"He looks good," Mollie called from where she was leaning against the arena fence, standing between Chip and Eric.

Looks like Mollie has two boys on the string, Shay thought as she rode back to Cherokee's stall. She was combing Cherokee's tail when her three friends joined her. This was the time Shay always hated. The waiting for her event to be called. Eric brought her an entry number and pinned it to the back of her coat. That took a little time, but mostly they waited.

After a while the boys went to the refreshment stand for Cokes, and Shay welcomed the chance to talk to Mollie privately.

"Didn't know Chip was interested in horse shows, Mol."

"But suddenly he is." Mollie beamed. "Nothing like a little competition to whet a guy's interest, right?"

"You mean Eric? Chip's jealous of Eric?"

"I wouldn't put it that strongly, but the word got around that Eric and I were at the D&D last Wednesday. I've noticed that Chip's been around a lot more ever since."

Shay smiled, pleased because Mollie was pleased. "Mol, whether I win a trophy or not, I'm going to celebrate this show by having that slumber party you were talking about. How about Sunday night? Just you and me and Beth and Sue."

"Sounds great, Shay. But will we be in any shape to go to school the next day?"

"Sure. We won't stay up talking *all* night. Anyway, on Monday we just have to show up to get our report cards."

When the boys returned, they sipped their drinks and watched Pony Lead-in, where parents led toddlers around the ring as they sat on their ponies. Then there was the Walk-Trot event for five- to eight-year-olds. After that they watched Pole Bending and a jumping event.

"Junior Western Pleasure," the announcer called over the loudspeaker. "Will all the participants for Junior Western Pleasure line up at the gate, please?"

"There you go," Eric said. "Good luck, Shay!"

"We're rooting for you, Shay," Chip said. "Keep cool."

Shay adjusted her hat and sat straight in the saddle. Heels down. Toes up. Left hand across her lap. Right hand controlling the reins. She scanned the makeshift bleachers until she saw her parents, smiled at them. Then she kept her attention on Cherokee and the other riders. She didn't want to see Towe, yet she could almost feel him watching her.

When all the entrants were in the ring, they walked their horses until the announcer called instructions.

"Trot your horses. Trot your horses, please."

Shay urged Cherokee to an easy trot, and they circled the ring twice. Was the judge watching her? She couldn't be sure. And it was poor form to look. How could he watch everyone? There were at least twenty riders in the ring.

"Reverse and canter," the announcer called. "Reverse your horses and canter, please."

Shay signaled the reverse and canter, and Cherokee

obeyed, smoothly, flawlessly. Had the judge noticed? Shay tried not to believe that judges noticed only mistakes and never noticed a correct performance. But sometimes it seemed that way. Today she had made no mistakes so far.

"Stop your horses, please. Stop your horses."

Shay signaled. Cherokee came to a perfect stop and stood steady. She held her breath. If only a fly didn't choose this moment to bite a leg, a rump. But Cherokee held firm.

"Canter, please," the announcer called. "Canter your horses."

Round and round the ring they went. How many times? Shay lost count. Then the judge began to motion riders to the center of the arena. After the first five were chosen, she felt her heart do a nose dive to her boots. The winners had been selected, and she wasn't among them! She was tempted to relax, but past training made her hold her show stance and keep riding until she heard other instructions.

"The riders in the center of the ring will please exit by the gate," the announcer called. "All riders in the center, please exit."

Shay's heart pounded. She hadn't lost! Not yet. The judge had been thinning out the contestants, getting rid of the ones he wasn't seriously considering. Shay rode with more determination than ever until only five riders remained in the ring. Five. At least she had won something. Again she was holding her breath. Now the judge called the riders to the center one by one. And she was last to be called. What did it mean? Was she the trophy winner? Or had she won the fifth-place ribbon? She listened as the judge began calling out names.

"Mike Donahue, fifth place."

Mike rode to the judge and accepted his ribbon.

After that the rest of the names were a blur in Shay's ears and her mind until she heard her own name, heard the cheers that almost drowned out the judge's voice.

"Shay Stuart. Trophy winner for Junior Western Pleasure."

Shay rode toward the judge. She stopped only long enough to accept the golden horse mounted on the polished walnut base and the blue ribbon that was also a part of the prize.

"Thank you, sir," she said.

"Good job, Shay," the judge replied. "A winner of a girl on a winner of a horse."

And the tears were coming again, only this time they were tears of pure happiness. She had won for Eric. And for Cherokee. And for herself. *A winner of a girl.* That's what the judge had said.

Now, as she left the ring, people crowded around to congratulate her. She dismounted, and Eric took the reins as she accepted a hug from her parents, backslaps from Mollie and Sue and Beth.

"Good ride, Shay."

When she heard Towe's voice, she thought for a moment that she might fall apart, but she didn't. Instead, she looked him in the eye and smiled. "Thanks, Towe. But it was Cherokee who did the really hard work. Eric's trained him so well!"

The announcer began calling the next event, and the crowd around Shay broke up as people gathered again around the arena fence.

"I'm really proud of you, Shay," Eric said. "I knew you were a good rider, but that performance was

. . . well, it was just perfect. And you had a lot of competition, too.''

"I had to be good, Eric. There was so much at stake.''

"We haven't talked about the awards dinner that follows the show tonight, Shay. I wish you'd go with me.''

Shay didn't even hesitate. "I'd love to go with you.'' She said the words and she meant them.

They walked Cherokee back to his stall, unsaddled him, brushed him down. Then, when they were finished, Shay picked up the trophy.

"Eric, I want you to have this. It'll go down on the official club record that I won it, and I'll need that credit if I have any chance of winning the right to represent the club at the state fair. But I want you to keep the trophy, you and Cherokee.''

"But it'll have your name engraved on it. They do that in a ceremony at the banquet tonight.''

"Good. I like the idea of you having a trophy with my name engraved on it.''

"Do you, really?'' Eric was looking at her, smiling at her in a way she had never seen him smile before, as if she were the only person in the world. But he didn't wait for her reply.

"If I accept the trophy, then you should accept something in return.''

"I could keep the ribbon.''

"Something more than that.'' Eric smiled down at her again, and before she could say anything, he drew her close and kissed her gently. She closed her eyes, enjoying the kiss, and when she opened them again, it was as if her whole world had changed.

She would always remember Towe Williams, but now

he was just a normal-sized memory in her mind. He was a nice guy she had known once a long time ago. Suddenly the world seemed very large. There were a lot of people in it. Towe Williams. Randy Russell. Eric Chapin.

And right now Eric Chapin was the person who interested her most. She watched the way the cleft in his chin deepened when he smiled. Yes, she was sure of it. She would always remember his smile.

6 brand new Silhouette Romance novels yours for 15 days–Free!

If you enjoyed this Silhouette First Love, and would like to move on to even more thrilling, satisfying stories then Silhouette Romances are for you. Enjoy the challenges, conflicts, and joys of love. Sensitive heroines will enchant you—powerful heroes will delight you as they sweep you off to adventures around the world.

6 Silhouette Romances, free for 15 days!

We'll send you 6 new Silhouette Romances to keep for 15 days, absolutely free! If you decide not to keep them, send them back to us. You pay nothing.

FREE HOME DELIVERY. But if you enjoy them as much as we think you will, keep them by paying the invoice enclosed with your free trial shipment. You'll then automatically become a member of the Silhouette Book Club and receive 6 more new Silhouette romances every month.

There is no minimum number of books to buy and you can cancel at any time.

First Love from Silhouette

Look for These
New First Love Romances from
Silhouette Books Next Month

A Boy To Dream About
Lisa Quinn

From the moment the dynamic young actor,
Casey Dewitt, stepped on stage, Michelle fell
under his spell. She was sure that his golden
hair and turquoise eyes would forever
enchant her. At last she would meet the boy
of her dreams.

For The Love Of Lori
Veronica Ladd

Andy and Lori had been neighbors and
friends since kindergarten. Yet when they
exchanged their first kiss, everything
changed. Would they ever be friends again?
Or should they risk the bittersweet
adventure of a first romance?

READERS' COMMENTS ON FIRST LOVE BOOKS

"I am very pleased with the First Love Books by Silhouette. Thank you for making a book that I can enjoy."

—G.O.*, Indianapolis, IN

"I just want you to know that I love the Silhouette First Love Books. They put me in a happy mood. Please don't stop selling them!"

—M.H.*, Victorville, CA

"I loved the First Love book that I read. It was great! I loved every single page of it. I plan to read many more of them."

—R.B.*, Picayune, MS

* names available upon request